DEEP OVERSTOCK

#16: Superheroes
April 2022

> "For me, Superman's greatest contribution has never been the superhero part: it's the Clark Kent part – the idea that any of us, in all our ordinariness, can change the world."
>
> *Brad Meltzer*

GN - SUPERHERO/SERIES

Editorial

Editors-In-Chief: Mickey Collins & Robert Eversmann

Managing Editors: Michael Santiago & Z.B. Wagman

Poetry: Jihye Shin

Prose: Michael Santiago & Z.B. Wagman

Additional Copyediting: Melissa Kerman

Cover by Viviann Ruiz

Contact: editors@deepoverstock.com
  deepoverstock.com

On the Shelves

7 Villanelle by Lucy Jayes

8 Don't Steal a Kiss from a Queen by Rob D. Smith

12 The Man Made of Stone by Ben Crowley

13 A superhero's contemplation by Wit Lee

15 Superbaby by Patricia Dutt

18 Among the Heroic Super-Stars by Karla Linn Merrifield

19 Superhero by Gale Acuff

22 The Hooded Jackal by Avary Clemont

27 Lavender Dreams by Audra Burwell

29 The Invincible Bastard by Michael Santiago

37 Vin by "doug"

38 I Can Be Your Hero Baby by Bob Selcrosse

39 On Loan from Sky by Phyllis Hemann

41 Spinsters by Kate Falvey

43 The Neighborhood Watch by Maev Barba

52 Requiem for a Radicalized Superman by CJ Huntington

54 You're Almost a Super Hero, Dad by Lynette G. Esposito

56 Hell is Empty and My Daughter Saves the Day by Kate Falvey

57 The Chocolate Drop by Aurora Lewis

63 Damien Strong by Vincent A. Alascia

67 Annie Rescues Herself by Kate Falvey

68 Everything I learned in life I learned twice by Alex Werner

69 How Joe "The Nose" Mulligan Survived 2020 by Jen Mierisch

74 I'm a superstar, and super high, but superhero? by Timothy Arliss OBrien

76 Unbreakable by Phyllis Hemann

77 My Mother, a Bionic by Anna Laura Falvey

78 The Powers of Outer Space by E.T. Starmann

84 What would I change in the world if I could? by Karla Linn Merrifield

85 The Little Villain That Could (But Could Only Do Good) by Eric Thralby

continued...

continued...

88 unrescuable by Lance Manion

91 A Public Service Announcement On Behalf of All Your Heroic Friends: by Nicholas Yandell

95 Superman by Gale Acuff

98 The Blood by Ben Crowley

101 Wrath of a Druidess by Audra Burwell

102 Nancy Drew Among the Amazons by Kate Falvey

104 No One is Wise -- Possible Magical Antidote #1

106 Mystique Exposed by Phyllis Hemann

108 The Golden Bureaucrat by Bob Selcrosse

109 Mother Flood by Anna Laura Falvey

110 Context is Everything by Karla Linn Merrifield

112 The Book-Stellar and Cat-a-log concept art unarchived by Mickey Collins

Letter from the Editors

Dearest Readers,

　　Look up in the sky! There, above the shelves and moving through the clouds. Is it a bird? A plane? Or some sort of bird-plane hybrid? No, it's the 16th issue of *Deep Overstock*: Superheroes!

　　Thank you for donning your capes, your masks, your tights, and saving us in this tumultuous time with your stories and poems on caped crusaders, vigilantism, and superpowers.

　　This issue is full of *BAM!* super men, *WHAM!* wonderous women, *ZAP!* a couple of babies, and it all adds up to a team-up of epic proportions. No villains could stop what you've created in these pages.

　　But now, put down that radioactive waste vat and continue looking up in the sky, for something's a-buzzing: it's bees! Beads? No, *bees* as in beekeeping the theme for Issue 17. So call us your queen and feed us that royal jelly called your submissions. We cannot wait to read what you send us, honey.

Yours, until felled by our arch-nemeses,

　　Deep Overstock Editors

Villanelle
by Lucy Jayes

We made a searching and fearless moral inventory of ourselves.

I have a superpower of my own
No matter how hard you knock
I can pretend no one is home
One thousand miles each way I have roamed
eyes forward like a yoked ox
I have a superpower of my own

Writing decay, anguish to loam
protected by a fence handmade of rocks
I can pretend no one is home

Blaming inheritance of my genome
believing there's time left on my clock
I have a superpower of my own
Memories hide in a catacomb
Among the tunnels my mind never walks
I can pretend no one is home

My only wish: to be left alone
place your messages into the box
I have a superpower of my own
I can pretend no one is home

Don't Steal a Kiss from a Queen
by Rob D. Smith

Queen Cobra leaped out the window on the 39th floor of the Derossett Building. It wasn't the tallest high-rise in Ark City but the fall would still kill her just the same. She snagged the line she had rappelled down earlier and moved deftly up it towards the roof. She moved preternaturally quick aided by the radioactive venom coursing through her bloodstream. She would need every drop of speed. He followed behind her.

At the lip of the roof, she flipped herself up over the edge almost dropping her shoulder bag with the Botha Diamond inside. The world's most perfect pink diamond. She swung the bag back snugly in place and exhaled. Stay loose but quick. She was fast. Her pursuer faster.

Dashing across the roof, she smiled at her equalizer hidden in a corner of the roof. Her Cobra glider. He may have the edge in speed but he couldn't sprout wings and fly after her. Just stand there and glare as she escaped. It was a damn sexy glare. She reached her glider and slid the harness on securing herself. From her peripheral vision, she caught a shadow pounce over the edge of the roof by her rappelling rope. She cursed herself for not cutting the line.

She stood wobbling the glider into launch position. Forward momentum achieved. Escape was just feet away when five claws ripped through the glider's canvas wing. Another sharp-clawed hand reached through the tear in the wing for her. She danced out of the harness rigging and gave the damaged glider a flip entangling her nemesis inside. She took a defensive posture as she checked for a backup exit.

The frame of the glider snapped apart revealing the Mongoose in his brindle patterned costume. The subtle stripes were dark and irregular. By contrast, her sleek form-fitting suit was iridescent green when she turned in the midnight moon. She pulled back the hood which helped resemble her cobra namesake.

"I'm not giving it back, Perry."

He growled and his eyes darted side to side.

"Relax. There are no eyes or ears on this roof. Just this lovely diamond between us." She patted her bag.

"Put it back, Miranda. Put it back and we can go back to being…"

"Being what exactly?" A coy smile revealing her two sharp fangs.

"Whatever you want to call it."

"Oh, Mister Control is allowing me to name what our relationship was." She pulled her right foot back a little.

He reached out his clawed hand. "You can… We can change. Just hand over the diamond."

She pirouetted away from his hand. "Who said I wanted to change?"

He dropped his hand. His shoulders too. "Queen Cobra is impulsive and dangerous. That's not your true nature. Miranda is kind, charitable, and uncompromisingly smart."

She spun closer to him then away and laughed. "I am all that and more. All our time together and the great Mongoose never learned anything about my true nature."

He didn't like to be mocked. He certainly didn't like to be laughed at. "Give me the diamond."

"Or?" She grinned across the roof to her ex-lover.

He rolled his broad shoulders. "I take it."

"A last dance then."

She pulled up her hood and he was already behind her

slashing at her shoulder bag strap. She slithered away just in time to evade his grasp. A sharp shin kick to his thick thigh. Muscle like armor. He tried to encircle her with his arms. A drop with a roll created some space between them. She flung three Cobra-rangs from her utility belt at Mongoose. He dodged two but one stuck in his chest.

He looked down at the sharp metal snake embedded in his flesh. A pluck with his fingers and it was out. He rubbed the blood between his fingertips and squinted his hunter eyes. "Why do you fight me?"

"Why do you chase me?"

She hadn't noticed him setting his feet and the ungodly fast lunge caught her off guard. His tackle bowled her over. She tucked them both into a roll leading them back to their feet but now in his unbreakable embrace. They were at the edge of the high rise. Wind whipping across their bodies. Eye to eye. Their breath on each other's cheek.

"I chase because you steal." His lips brushed hers as he spoke and they kissed.

The kiss was tenderly backlit with passion. Their lips parted. The kiss lingered then Queen Cobra bit his lip hard injecting venom from her fangs. He swung his head away from her attack and pushed her to the ground. His face was like a wounded child.

"I fight because you want to cage me."

He dabbed at his already swollen lip. A bit of a stagger as the radioactive venom coursed through his veins. He leaned his ass back onto the edge of the roof. "This only delays our dance. My immunity will shrug this off soon. It won't stop me."

She stood up and weaved her way to him placing her hands on his knees. She leaned in with a frown. "No, it won't darling but this fall will."

She grabbed ahold of his brindle fur costume behind the knees and flipped him over the edge. At the lip the city lights reflected on her iridescent scaled body-suit, she stared down at the plummeting protector of Ark City. He didn't scream on the way down. His nature wouldn't let him. She didn't cry for the same reason.

The Man Made of Stone
by Ben Crowley

There are few superheroes as ancient as The Man Made of Stone, for he has seen every shade the villains of evil can make bubble and boil from the depthless undying center of earth, from which all evil springs.

It burns at 9,392° Fahrenheit, the earth's core. It is from this molten evil pumice, obsidian, granite, quartz shot to the surface of the earth like billion-year missiles. It is from this molten evil we too were blessed one summer with The Man Made of Stone.

The Man Made of Stone's two burning eyes cast judgment on us all.

There is no rest for the Man Made of Stone.

On Monday, he sees a woman abandon her baby to rats.

On Tuesday, it rains and a love triangle overdose.

On Friday, a man gives his mother to the alley because her brain no longer works.

Nothing escapes The Man Made of Stone, for he has seen it all and will go on for eternity seeing it all, casting judgment on us all from those two burning eyes.

A superhero's contemplation
by Wit Lee

I
There're wheels of light rolling in the sky
There're no wheels of light rolling in the sky

Eyes full of patients
Superheros
Entrances everywhere
No exit

II
Lying alone in bed
Complete the ceremony of a suffering
Superhero
This accidental solemnity
Only poetry can witness
Arise of this era—
Insert the gear into the broken backbone
Implant chips into the dying brain
Store, copy, paste and format
Love, hate, hope, desperate
——what a perfect operation!
Come to birth another patient, or superhero
Manipulate data to form a human-like
Voice. What a beautiful voice!
Hallelujah!
Release the mushroom flame with the button
Up, up

You——a superhero, or a patient
Of this era!

III
Magical world, cars drunk wheels in crowd
Wheat scavenges food in cities
House abandones walls

Bat suckes and eats this
Crazy world

IV

The sky rides on a bird
It needs a mount
Ride, ride
Like a superhero
Forward
Forward,will there be a new hometown
Beyond this fake world?

V

Ceremony is over
Poetry bails its head from
Abyss of dust
Eyes kneels down to the sky
Wind faces the crying wall
Contemplating, clouds are attached to
The elephant's feet, mouths are full of thorns
And eyes are fulfilled with fogs

VI

There is a hometown in the sky
There is no hometown in the sky
Smokes of the earth piled up in
Your, my, everyone's throat
Up and up, stairs of desire
Rotating, a superhero wandering between
Heaven and hell
Entrances everywhere
No exit

Superbaby
by Patricia Dutt

The new parents declined every social invitation two weeks before traveling and shopped for groceries only late at night. When it was time, they took the train at off-hours to a hotel with stringent safety protocols, and made sure their international airline had excellent air purification procedures. They were careful, careful, careful to stay six feet apart from strangers in all public spaces and wore double, high-tech masks. Thus they successfully schlepped the baby, who was eight-months-old, across an ocean and over two continents, subjecting him to heights of 33,000 feet for hours on end then landing in a sleepy US airport (planned) right before an unprecedented number of holiday flights were cancelled (not planned). This all during a surging pandemic. When they arrived at their final destination – a small city in central New York where the new mother's mother lived – tales were told about this remarkable baby: how he smiled and laughed, not only ate but loved broccoli, crawled backward (not yet forward), flipped over and even waved his tiny hands in the air while imprisoned in the high chair -- sign language for "All done!" For the most part, however, superbaby regarded the wide, wide world with curiosity. "Nothing is ever going to stop this baby," the young mother declared.

Feeling that they were at the top of their game, the parents went out for a local craft beer, the first alcohol in nearly 18 months for the new mother. The next morning, after getting up three times to nurse, as the mother was changing the baby who was not quite at the bed edge but close to it, the baby executed another feat: he flipped over twice and so rapidly that before he belly-flopped onto the hard floor the mother barely caught his look of surprise: How could you let this happen to me? Me? A shriek shook the house as superbaby impacted the wood floor. It unhinged the mother, who shook the house with her own agglomeration of shrieks. The husband tore out of the bathroom with soap on his face and everyone was crying. And the baby became more enraged by the second.

After calling the hospital for expert advice and a virtual pat on the shoulder, the new parents crept about in defeat and guilt. Even when the baby smiled at them, they sadly smiled back, knowing they had failed superbaby. The baby did his usual gooing and gaaing and played with his toys as if they possessed mystical powers that only superbaby could unleash. He performed his newly acquired feat—flipping -- and giggled whenever successful, but such gymnastics were now highly restricted: only on the carpeted floor!

The parents removed their socks before descending the wood stairs with the baby, they did not give him any broccoli lest the gag reflex suddenly fail. They themselves had no appetite. They did not allow him to play unmonitored, in fact, at night, one of them always slept in the same room as superbaby. The mother imagined the baby would grow up and blame her for the rest of her life for those two seconds of inattention because she wanted to have one beer. Her son will keep secrets from her, like those concerning his high school girlfriends he cavalierly impregnated and consequently denied responsibility for. Then he will drop out of his private, expensive college mid-semester and never ever be able to rise early enough to work at a real job, so he'll become some kind of drug kingpin/addict/cult leader who will prey upon the young and innocent. He will never visit his parents during the holidays.

This, the new mother knew.

But the new parents stupidly ran out of diapers, and the older mother was gone somewhere, so the parents carefully installed the baby in his winter suit, positioned his little hattie so his tiny ears would not get cold, made sure his car seat was secure, covered him with a blanket, and drove at 10 miles-an-hour to the irritation of the long line of drivers behind them to the grocery store. Once there, the parents secured the baby in the front pack carrier on the father (the mother could not trust herself: she might fall) and the three of them, masked and with squirts of hand sanitizer, entered the grocery store and made a bee-line for the baby section. As the parents scanned the shelves, the mother noticed a curly-haired girl, a toddler, squeezing a duck.

"Quack, quack," the duck said.

The little girl laughed back and kept squeezing the duck, and the duck responded: they were like long-time chums, trading observations about the habits of toddlers and ducks. Suddenly the store's seasonal background music was interrupted by an announcement: "There is a two-year old girl, curly brown hair, brown eyes, wearing a red coat. Her mother is looking for her!" Everyone heard the frantic mother, presumably behind the serious announcer, crying: "Clara! Clara! Where are you, honey?"

The little girl's brown eyes widened, and the parents escorted Clara to the Customer Service Center where the frantic mother was wringing her hands, her eyes wet with tears, and as soon as the little girl saw her mother, she started bawling. They hugged and howled together and people paused their serious shopping expeditions and gave the mother a comforting elbow (no pats on the back) and exclaimed: "How wonderful! How sweet! What a lovely, darling girl! I like a story with a happy ending!"

The parents looked at one other, then back to the fanatical mother, still blubbering away.

The new mother said: "Give me the baby." So the father strapped the baby onto her, and then they bought their favorite foods: sushi, and a salad bowl with extra edamame and blue cheese. And broccoli, of course, for superbaby.

Among the Heroic Super-Stars

by Karla Linn Merrifield

To Cetus I pray:
Grant me the gene memories
of Earth's singing whales.

The Pleiades yield
magical capacity
to ancient wishes.

Orion eases
modern insecurities;
I grow more primal.

Ursa roars wildest
grammars of animacy
that I may bear grief.

From Virgo's house
comes the polemical fist
of stars, of stardust.

Superhero
by Gale Acuff

I can buy two comics for a quarter
at the druggist near the department store
next to the restaurant where we eat out
almost every Friday night. '66
it is, and I'm just ten; my allowance
is twenty-five cents a week. I blow it
on superheroes. I'm a good student,
bring home A's and B's, and am Captain
of the School Safety Patrol. I'm what you call
responsible. But on weekends I'm free
to do almost anything I want to,
so I read comic books, play with the dog,
ride my bike, play baseball or football or
basketball--it depends on the season,
and we have four of them here in Georgia.

In the drug store I stand before the rack
of magazines. Below them, the comics.
I'm looking for *Superman* and *Batman*,
Flash, *Green Lantern*, Wonder Woman, *Atom*,
Hawkman--if I can find the Justice League
then I have them all for the price of one,
and watch them work together to defeat
evil, which isn't much of a problem

in our town, though I'm still too young to know
that crime can pay, and that politics
is organized crime, but somehow legal.
And we haven't lost in Vietnam yet,
Nixon's not President, and LBJ
can still talk-up the Great Society.
But in the comic books evil never wins
but still gives goodness one heck of a fight.
I like it when things begin wrong but end

right. Me, I don't know much about failure
--enough to know I don't want to be one.

Fight evil and you can't go wrong, even
if you're killed--you're a hero and that's heaps
better than being alive and nothing.
Look at Ferro Lad, of the Legion of
Super-Heroes: he gave his life to save
the galaxy--it says so right there on
his statue. What a guy, and he doesn't
even exist. It's a head-scratcher, though
--he's alive somehow (forget that he's dead)
among the four-colors and drawings and
words in word-balloons and staples and ink
in my copy of *Adventure Comics*,
but the nearest I can come to know him
is by reading the story; without it

I'm nothing to him, only make-believe.
But in my collection of the Legion
I'm sort of an honorary member
whenever I read along. So which world
is real? I wonder if the Legionnaires
pass around a comic book about me
and turn the pages to see how I pan
out. I hope I won't be canceled, at least
not for a very long time. Who knows but
that I'm a hero to those teenagers
of the thirtieth century? And this,
my mild-mannered life in Marietta,
Georgia, is just the one they've given me

by believing. When Monday morning comes,
I've got to go to school again. I know
someone's watching me--in church they say it's
God, but I think it's the eyes of readers
following my exploits. They're happy that
I don't give up, and hustle on the field
and make good marks and obey my parents
at least most of the time and clean my plate
and make my bed and take out the garbage
and wash the car and feed the dog and clean
out the garage and mow the grass and sweep
the porch and pick up my clothes and say Grace.
I must really be something else to them.
And when I die of old age I'll be well

-thumbed, but still a collector's item, Poor or Fair or Good or Fine or Near-mint or Mint condition. But still a classic.

The Hooded Jackal
by Avary Clemont

I used to be just a girl from a poor home in Brazil, the nerd everyone picked on, the girl everyone called unwanted, but now they call me a hero. Hello, my name is Camilla. I was chosen by a few Egyptian gods to protect humanity against demons and other unworldly monsters. I have spent the last three months fighting bad guys and getting my butt beat by villains like Set, the god of war. But no matter how many times I get beat down, I always manage to get back up. I'm getting ahead of myself. Let's go back to where it all started...

"Isn't Egypt beautiful, Camilla?"

"Yeah, Mom, the harsh sun and hot sand are so lovely."

"Camilla, Egypt is more than sun and sand. It's about culture and history."

"I know, Mom."

Once we arrived at the unnamed temple, my mom and I put up our tents. I started settling in for the night when I heard my mom and the lead archaeologist arguing about money. I ignored them and pulled out my journal. I sat in my tent writing theories about what could be in this new temple. Who did it belong to? Lost in thought, I didn't notice the sun slowly setting until my mother walked into my tent and wished me a good night. I put my journal into my backpack and curled up on my air mattress. I dreamed of sandstorms and adventures until I awoke to a voice calling out to me. I got up from my bed and walked out of my tent.

"Hello, Mom?"

The voice heightened.

"Camilla, come into the temple."

Why was the temple calling to me? I started walking toward the temple. Once inside, a beam of light led me safely through the traps and down many stairs.

"Hey, voice guy, where are you taking me?"

The voice didn't respond. I continued to follow the mystical light down the winding staircase until we reached a large room. Scratched-out hieroglyphics covered the walls and silk clothing scattered around.

"Camilla, the amulet...Take the amulet."

I looked around the room before I spotted an old desk-like piece of furniture. Something gold laid upon it, surrounded by red silk. I quickly approached the desk and grabbed the gold item. It was a beautiful gold necklace that had four symbols engraved on it. The necklace looked brand new, untouched by time, and unharmed by the sand around it. I slipped the amulet over my head and let it fall onto my chest. All of a sudden a sandstorm erupted. The cold sand swirled around the room as multiple voices started speaking. I closed my eyes and fell to the ground, curling up in a ball with my hands over my head. After a while the sand settled down and the voices stopped. I slowly opened my eyes but, before I could stand up and check my surroundings, a deep voice came from behind me.

"Hello, tiny earth child."

I hesitantly turned around to see Osiris the god of the underworld standing behind me. I jumped to my feet as sweat dripped from my forehead. I was horrified. What had I just unleashed?

"H...H...Hello lord of the underworld."

I could feel my heart attempting to jump out of my body.

"Please child, call me Osiris. All that formal nonsense is unneeded."

"Yes sir...I mean Osiris."

The lord of death walked over to me and put his hand on my shoulder. He asked me to look into his eyes. Although I was fearful I mustered up the strength to look at him. When our eyes met, I started seeing flashbacks of my life, the good and the bad all my thoughts and feeling rushing through me like a raging waterfall.

"...stop..."

"Just a little more earth child."

As memory after memory flooded my mind, I started to feel a crushing sense of agony start to creep up on me, I hadn't felt this way In a long time. I started begging him to stop but he keep pushing into my past until he found it the root of my suffering the memory that made me who I am today: my father's murder. He broke eye contact with me as I fell to my knees screaming in pain. My eyes flooded with tears.

"You try to fill the void by helping people?"

"...I couldn't save him, it's all my fault I wasn't brave enough!"

I wiped my face off with one of the old silk fabrics that were laying on the ground.

"A broken soul with a heart of pure silk. How poetic. Wouldn't you say, Osiris?"

This voice was different. It wasn't as deep, I looked up and to my surprise, there stood Anubis the god of spirits.

"Please don't look into my eyes."

He smiled at me before walking over to me.

"No need to be wary of me. I am no threat."

He helped me up and then walked toward Osiris.

"If you don't mind me asking...why are you guys here?" I said through sad sniffles.

Osiris turned to me.

"All will be revealed once my son arrives."

I sighed and walked over to the back wall of the room. Whoever scratched out these hieroglyphs must have been enraged, but why? Before I could ponder the question a loud screech came from outside the room.

A tall falcon walks into the room, he eyes me up and down before looking at his father.

"This is the human?"

"Yes, Horus. She is the one Ra prophesied."

I walked over to them.

"Prophesied? Wait Ra the god of Egypt's creation?"

"Yes, you see Ra had a dream many weeks ago about a girl pure of heart that would protect humanity, from hellish beings and the one we call Set."

"The god of war."

"You are very well versed in Egyptian mythology."

"Well my mom is an archaeologist. We have lots of..."

"I'm sorry to interrupt but I have to raise the morning star soon, so can we get this over with?"

"Yes, of course."

Horus pulled out an old book from his Shendyt and handed it to me.

"What is this?"

"It's the book of the dead."

I flipped through the pages before closing the book and looking back up at Horus.

"So, is it too late to tell you I can't read Egyptian?"

"Don't worry child. The amulet will help with that."

"We must now leave you, but do not fret. We will always be here to guide you."

And with those last words, Horus flew me out of the temple and set me back in my tent. From that day on I have been protecting humans from themselves and demons.

Lavender Dreams
by Audra Burwell

Tumbling through cotton candy clouds,
I thread my fingers between gossamer
Strands of pale pink and baby blue
Soft as spider's silk, wrapping around
My pinky, an ethereal ribbon of light.
Body flailing, caught in free-fall,
I surrender to gravity's demands,
Letting moisture pool upon my lashes
Lavender crystals nestled above my eyes,
I inhale invisible capsules of air,
Feeling bubbles of oxygen caress
The lining of my slender throat.
Imaginary lines guide me through
The marmalade horizon, a compass
Fixed upon my destiny, hidden,
Beneath clouds of taffeta and velvet,
Draped across the sky like a grand
Curtain obscuring the celestial ball
Materializing high in the heavens.
My fingers numbed from the wintry
Kiss of lingering nimbus shadows,
Tangle themselves in the tether,
Fixed to my harness of deliverance.
A gentle tug, easing the lever open,
And I am hurtled against the sky
Arms outstretched like wings of
Smoke and shadow, blackening
The fiery glow of the setting sun.
Ballooning above my head, patches
Of lilac and indigo flutter as my
Parachute unfurls the shell of its
Mushroom canopy, nylon cords,
Connecting me like a marionette.
Gliding effortlessly through the,
Diminishing atmosphere, I breathe
In rays of pale blue, feeling them
Tickle the oscillating membrane

Of my lungs, like a pale feather,
Trapped by the cyclone of a storm.
Ridges of land unfold rapidly below,
Canyons carved from the bones of
Buried ancestors sleeping beneath
Rocks painted red and gold.
Squeezing my frozen eyelids shut,
I steel myself for Earth's fatal impact
Only to feel the embrace of sun-baked
Soil licking my trembling toes, as
They sink into sand as gold as dawn.
Flashes of lilac and lavender tease
My peripheral view, as my parachute
Pools behind me, a deflated carcass
Retired from the liberation of the sky.
Gazing heavenward, a fervent longing
Lingers in my chest, beckoning me to
Once more seek that forbidden freedom.

The Invincible Bastard
by Michael Santiago

  The resounding, deafening cries rattled the interior panels within the cylindrical titanium rotunda. Screams emanated through the adjacent halls while blinding rays of teal light flooded the structure. The temperature dropped and increased without notice, and the entire floor reverberated as the screaming ensued, heightening in pitch. Such was the routine for Logan, former hero and figurehead of the Vindication.

  Across the room, a tempered glass box elevated 40 feet off the ground housed the control room for the central dome. Inside, lab coats operated panels intended to quell the trapped titan. Head Chief Monroe, the overseer, pressed a large, flat button to initiate a loudspeaker inside the dome and softly stated, "Do you understand the composition of the human body, Logan? An intricate, interwoven network of fibrous tissue confining muscle to bone and bone to bone. The myocardium beating and pulsing blood, delivering oxygen and vital nutrients to every intentionally placed organ. With a cerebrum firing synapses at unfathomable velocity."

  As Monroe continued to speak, Logan sat up and fixated his attention, gazing upon the glass box with intensity. His feet planted firmly on the glossed marble tile. He stared at Monroe with utter hatred, and the vibrant teal hue in his eyes grew brighter. An enormous shockwave rattled the interior as he began screaming, rippling the panels across the ceiling. And then, launching a teal beam from his eyes, aimed directly at Monroe, he grew angrier. And, to no avail, the barricaded encasement remained intact against his calamitous tantrum.

  "Now, imagine a god walking among such delicate, fragile forms. A whisper would be enough to decimate organic life into a pile of viscous goo. A single twitch capable of obliterating cities. A mere mental breakdown is enough to disrupt the forces which adhere to natural law. Absolute decimation. Human extinction. All within your grasp, Atlas. If you so willed it," Monroe stated.

Rage compounded and conflated within Logan as he recalled his moniker, Atlas. Aware his ocular photon blast could not crack the structure; he began pounding his hands impetuously onto the marble floor. Each thud rippled and splintered the surface, yet titanium sheathed the entire dome. Then, he placed each hand onto the ground and began to fluctuate the temperature from a scorching 1,800 degrees Fahrenheit to -100 degrees below zero. Neither range was enough to melt or shatter the prison. The scope of his ability was a spectacle on display, with every show of power solidifying the position of Monroe's stranglehold.

Once more, he spoke, "And as the world cheered and applauded your arrival, your ego proliferated. The world embraced you for the nobility you masqueraded, not for the calloused heroic antics that marginalized you from the rest of your team. However, those who inhibit logic knew something like you could not be contained. That it was simply time abiding your true nature. You do remember your true nature, Atlas?"

Sapped and frustrated, Logan sat onto the floor, locking a steely-eyed leer with Monroe.

"It was Tuesday. A gaggle of patrons embraced you and your Vindication. Do you even remember them? Those you once called friends," he said.

As Logan placed his head on his forearm, he spoke, "This parade of power you berate me with is no different than the one of which you are about to speak, you insignificant peon. Yes, I remember that little show and those sycophants."

"Care to tell?" he asked.

"Rosenberg. Calling upon us one by one from behind a curtain like a band of circus freaks. Showboating us. So, yes, I remember that day well along with those super fucks," Logan shouted.

"Can you describe that day to me, Atlas?" he inquired.

Shifting his gaze back to Monroe, he stood up and began to speak, "we had just located a white supremacist group who was responsible for the bombings of several black churches on the southside of Chicago. The formerly living mayor, Rosenberg, threw this little parade to celebrate what the Vindication had done to save the city. One by one, we marched on stage to make our required appearances when shit like this happened. Star Child, Atom of Dawn, Credence, War Siren, and Serpentine were there, but that band of stupid fucks never pulled their weight."

"Is that why you killed them that day, too? Because you felt you were carrying the team single handedly?" he provoked.

"Is this a joke? Rosenberg set up these terrorist events to pull votes. Oh, and that little ordeal at the church, well, I killed everyone there, by myself. If you want the real story, Star Child was banging War Siren in the alley outside the church, Credence was busy marketing himself on social media, and Atom of Dawn and Serpentine could not shut up about the results of Wimbledon. I mean, arguing over tennis when on the job? I took out everyone in that church, alone," Logan uttered.

"And that was enough to massacre them in front of a relished crowd of supporters?" he prodded.

Logan grew increasingly furious and yelled, "War Siren was my fucking girlfriend, and Star Child was my best friend and both betrayed me, so, yes, I lasered them in half in front of the crowd. Credence was a pompous, superficial flatterer who never did a single heroic thing yet took credit for my actions. Atom of Dawn had the most obnoxious ability to rearrange atomic structures ONLY at dawn. What kind of power limits you to a single time of the day? Also, Serpentine was what? 2,000 years old? It was her time. Aside from that, they were scheming, figuring out how to kill me, as they were terrified of my abilities. Oh, and before I forget, I was Rosenberg's puppet. So, I had enough and flexed my abilities a little. The crowd was an accident. They were collateral damage. They shouldn't have even been there."

"This is how you justify your narcissism? Through ill-equipped, inabilities of those around you? Blaming others for the actions that transpired by your hand?" he questioned.

"Don't you… don't you dare label me that. She used to project that same thing onto me, but I was just a child." Logan yelled.

"Who are you referring to?" he asked.

As Logan's gaze shifted downward, a glint of remorse compounded with sadness skewed the maniacal, frenetic state by which he was consumed. Dropping his arms to his waist and focusing on the floor, a tear plummeted to the titanium surface. He began to reflect on the question asked, forcing him to look within and dial back to the moments defining his upbringing.

Envisioning his youth, he recalled the myriad of abuse Clymene, his mother, doled out.

"You good for nothing, little shit. Get over here! I told you that you could not just say whatever you wanted! This is my house, and I demand respect. It will be given to me one way or another or so help me, god," his mother screamed.

The nude adolescent Logan was kneeling on a bed of raw rice, with the pressure of the grains piercing his skin. Weeping silently, the cruelty exerted was unequivocal to his action, yet she only focused on raw rage. It satiated her agony with an unbroken cycle of abuse; she did not offer a reprieve for the young boy. Punishment in place of compassionate discourse formed the basis of his youth.

"Now get up. Put on your clothes, and the next time you give me a disrespectful look when I speak to you, it'll be worse," she shouted.

Clasping the ground, he pushed himself up as his knees were embedded with rice. A bloody trail of crimson despair followed Logan to his bed, and as he sat down, he wept in solitude, naked and afraid. These tears were not due to the pain inflicted upon him but for the person his mother was. Clymene shattered cemented ideals of how a true mother should be, but Logan still tried to justify the actions hurled toward him. His internal dialogue convinced him it was just and deserving. That he was exactly what his mother told him he was. The perpetuated anguish passed through the ages, with Logan as the passenger of her pain.

Before he could pull every grain from the wounds they formed, his mother yelled, "this rice and this pity party trail you left isn't going to clean itself." Sliding on his undergarments and grabbing a rag with dried blood, he began to clean the scarlet drops from the hardwood floor. Sweeping up the rice, he glanced at his mother as she spoke to herself aloud, regurgitating religious passages and further demeaning her offspring.

Pacing back and forth, gripping a crucifix around her neck, she muttered, "God, why did you give me a girl masquerading as a boy? He is lazy, disrespectful, useless, and acts like he is the one in charge. And then when I get mad, I am the bad mother. I'm tired of having to deal with such a disrespectful child."

"Logan… Logan, calm down," Monroe's voice echoed.

Once more, a teal hue emitted from his eyes as he began slamming his head into the titanium cell walls. "If it were not for her, I wouldn't be this fucked up. I didn't mean to kill anyone. I wanted to lead, be a hero, but I became exactly what she told me I was. It just never stopped. Until one day it did," Logan replied.

Smashing his skull against the interior, a flood of memories verbally poured out. He offered vague mentions of his abuse aloud as he said, "all of the times she berated me. She told me I was a girl because I did not carry my weight in the house like a man. She would then tell me to stop acting like a big tough man when I was silent. The back and forth. Forcing used bars of soap and jalapenos down my throat when I spoke against her abuse. Then she threw my recently deceased pet into the trash instead of burying it with me. The older I got, the more calloused I became until she threw me against the wall so hard my spine cracked, which was the first time I realized I was more than just a helpless child."

"Is that when Atlas emerged? When she threw you?" Monroe questioned.

Pulling back, he offered a single nod and said, "yes. I picked myself back up and looked right in her eyes as I scorched concaves through each eye socket. The years of anguish manifested into raw, unrelenting power."

"Atlas. Logan. You decimated the entire city. Murdered your comrades. Exerted godlike power onto innocent bystanders who offered you nothing but praise. This travesty cannot be misconstrued as a trauma response. You were a herald who wielded unfathomable capabilities, which instilled terror. You can't be allowed to do whatever you will, nor can you continue walking among us to commit such an act again," Monroe said.

Monroe backed from the panel and offered a stern nod to a man sitting at a switchboard, who then proceeded to push a series of buttons in sequence. The titanium encasement was not a prison; it was a death chamber, Logan's iron maiden. Toxic fumes spilled through a vent adjacent to his bed, and then he placed his hands onto the floor as rage consumed the unruly hero.

The temperature rose vigorously, eventually exceeding his initial limit of 1,800 degrees. The cell began to liquify around him and then he howled as the temperature output now surpassed the sun. Through the thick black plumes, globs of boiled titanium pooled around his feet. Inching each step forward, he raised his left fist and catapulted through the glass box above the room.

Looking at the lab coats drenched in fear, he said, "did you think you could kill me? Shame, you must not have given my dossier a thorough read. I cannot be killed. I'm invincible."

His hollow gaze-evoked dread as he demanded Monroe's

presence. Terror paralyzed the lab coats as not a single word was muttered. "Do you think this is a fucking game? Where is he?" Logan demanded.

Logan picked up one of the lab coats by the base of his skull and applied an insignificant amount of pressure, which was enough to combust the man's head. Splattering fragments of skull and cerebral goo across the room. "Now, will you tell me where he is?" Logan demanded.

The evincive titan gleaned upon every lab coat; his gaze jutted as the teal hue in his eyes began gleaming. Exerting his ocular blast, he tore flesh from sinew and ravaged the interior of the control room. A crimson brandishing coated the space. He took a few hollow steps forward and noticed a dossier on an adjacent console. Grabbing the file, he read to himself, "Project Lapetus: The Deity Destroyer.."

As he perused the document, he noticed an antiquated black and white photo dating to 1967. In the image, a chiseled, muscle-bound man was clasping onto the hands of what appeared to be his mother, Clymene, as they were both standing next to Monroe. They appeared gleeful as it was apparent that Clymene was pregnant. Behind them, an old Greek ruin littered the background

Unable to comprehend the imagery, he gazed upon the dossier once more and said, "I'm going to find you, dad, and you're going to tell me everything.

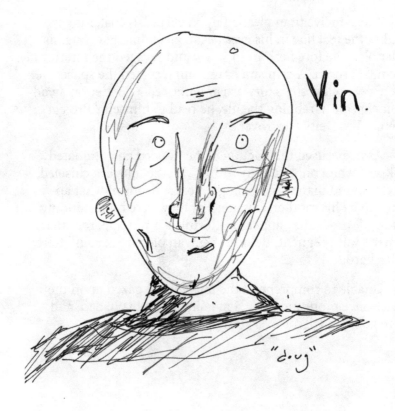

Vin
by "doug"

I wish I was Vin Diesel
The only bone I ever broke was a fucking tooth
Vin diesel drove a car out of one skyscraper into another
I'm so thin, my own family says I'll float away in the wind
I bet Vin has never questioned how much of a man he is

To be Vin Diesel must be nice
But I wonder how he feels
Do you think Vin is self-conscious ever?
Looking in the mirror,
Feeling disgusted?
Who fucking knows

I guess someone could just ask him
But we just want to know about his job
About the characters
And about the Heroes he portrays
I bet Vin doubts himself
I bet he doesn't like parts of his body too

I look in the mirror
I hate what I see
I definitely don't look like Vin Diesel
I only look like me
It's all I will ever look like

This is the part where I am supposed to say
"I always be me and that's okay"
I'm working on it, Vin
I may never look like him
But with time,
I will come to terms with myself

Just like Vin Diesel

I Can Be Your Hero Baby
by Bob Selcrosse

I have to admit to myself and therefore also to you: I am a baby inside. I work in an office. I have no illusions. But after punching out, after uncinching that tie, after sliding those slacks down the length of my regrettably adult-length shaven legs, I am nothing, if not a baby. Call me and I mean it anytime you need a pudgy love-button like me.

You may see me in the street with a briefcase, but under my suit it's just me and my nappy. My distress signal is a cry for hunger in the night. Wah! Like a lighted bat upon the wall, when I cry you'll know it's time to come and feed me. Just give me a call. I'll be there in *THE BABY MOBILE* also known as "The Stroller," a partially restored 1955 baby blue Nash Rambler. You will recognize it by its horn, which is also the cry of a baby.

You may think I do not count. That I do not belong here with a book full of heroes. But ask yourself, who else will save you, when you just need someone to need?

On Loan from Sky
by Phyllis Hemann

I possess
a lease agreement

40 some odd
pages

detailing

the story of my life
time as a heroine
on this planet.

No small print
only a straight
forward agreement

to bestow my talent
and treasure
to my fellow man

anointed
until my last breath
to instill my legend.

I'm at the point
in my contract
where I see my own
vulnerability.

Life roars by me,
a Ghost Rider blazing down
a deserted stretch of highway.

No amount of comic book
powers can halt the march
of days and stave off
the inevitable destination.

I retool my image
of heroic. Real
heroines don't mess
around with cinematic
perfection.

Spinsters
by Kate Falvey

II. One way of looking at it
Sever the notion of quest from blood
and you get girls, leastways if the blood
is othered and the quest is sticky with
swords and snares, beset with spiteful
nymphs and pitiless trials, fool's gold
guarded by dragon-fire, the road to
illuminant decency – or what passes as –
marked by split skulls, victors gloating
with vainglorious gore.

Women break open skeins in the dark,
hearth-flares dappling the cradles and
spindles, the medicinal tinctures steeping
in secret. Women whisper spells of
protection, weave warnings in threads of
rage and remorse, fly from story to story
on their blackthorn beliefs, brandishing
betony and witch's bells, concocting,
preserving death-defying lore.

II. Or

Women revel in blood,
desensitized from spilling so much of it.

They spin by the firesides,
enchanting the crestfallen flames.

They know who to blame
though often unexamined,

self-suppressing shame makes
them fawning in allegiance

to a basso profundo command
from the monster they married

ere sired by and instead
of slaying that particular trial,

they capitulate and cringe and
secretly conspire with each other

and the primeval elements
to withstand the practiced torments

of yet another everlasting wait,
blood spilling into stories,

clotting the quest with eons of ire,
a subtle, straitened fury, with guile

and clues for their daughters
who may one day breathe fire

while their mothers continue to spin
crafty defiance in their graves.

The Neighborhood Watch
by Maev Barba

The Neighborhood Watch was four people. I was one of those four people. I, like you or your mom, get up every morning and pull on my pants. I sit on the toilet. I brush my teeth. They call me The Tamer, or Toni, the Tamer. The joke is not lost on me, friends, no. My favorite animal is the tiger and I have some issues with anger. I'll admit it. And while I do not have superheroes, I do believe in superheroes. And that has made all the difference.

I say 'was' four people because only recently we lost our beloved Marlene.

Marlene went gray years ago, but every week dyed it pink–every shade of pink, even purples, of extremely deep or extremely light shades, sometimes even subtle blues, but never a combination.

We took bets on the color. When Ash and I arrived outside Marlene's house (Neighborhood Watch Headquarters) on Queens Lane at about the same time, we conspired along the walkway before we knocked upon her door. Ash always bet on purple. I always bet on pink.

When we went to identify the body after Marlene's alleged critical heart failure, her hair was a carnivalesque bubblegum pink.

Marlene was native Hawaiian. You might have called either of us fat, I don't know. I don't know your standards. I don't know your tastes. But I can run up a fire escape and jump over walls. I do not have a thigh gap unless I'm kicking your ass. Are you a bad man? Would you like that?

Marlene never hid in a name. To us she was always 'Marlene.' And she took names just for fun, changing her names and super-identities as flippantly as she did her crazy old-lady hair colors. These are what she called them herself. "Yes, Tomi, and do you know why I have dyed my hair a new shade of periwinkle?" she was known to have said to me. "Because there is a bad man. Around every corner. Inside every shadow. There is a bad man in all of our hearts. Pull them all up like worms from the dirt. I am the Pink Peregrine. And I will uproot them like worms."

She was a woman of limitless inspiration and care.

We met in her living room. The walls were full of small pictures of her generations of family. Marlene sat beside a Tiffany lamp, fanning herself with a wicker fan made of palm leaves, three of which were also provided for the three of us as well (although we seldom used them, as we lived in Detroit). It was a very small, compact living room, but it was perfectly cozy.

Ash and Gemini always sat on a small couch, and I sat in the armchair, compulsively eating from the plate of cheese squares on Ritz crackers on the coffee table between us. We sat and we talked. And we talked of The Neighborhood Watch.

Our powers weren't particularly strong. The mean streets of Detroit would stab us, tie us up in a bundle, and leave us by the trash to bleed out. But in our strange little neighborhood, we could make a real difference.

Gemini could split into two people like the Wonder Twins. They could not take on different shapes or forms, but could operate independently as two people, a boy and a girl. Gemini was always at Marlene's house before me and Incendiary. (We called her 'Ash,' though professionally she was 'Incendiary.') They were Marlene's niece and nephew, but, if I will say it honestly, I've never seen the two of them in the same room.

Marlene's powers too were suspect. Maybe she had no powers at all. Maybe she was just really good at listening to people. But she never was wrong.

"You've got potential, kid," she had said.

"What?" I said. I was forty and I was drunk in public before noon.

"You clean up your act. You come talk to me. There's something special about you."

I was hunched over a trash can looking up at her. Her lilac hair was spinning around like a pinwheel.

Marlene was my sponsor. She too had overcome that heavy beast of drinking, about fifteen years before. She told me I had something special inside me. I could not read the future, nor split into two people, nor burn houses down, nor fly like I wanted, but I was super nonetheless.

"I can see it," she said.

"What?" I said.

She stared at me from her armchair by her Tiffany lamp. "The *future*. And I know that you never get any powers. But I know, and I know this perhaps more, that you belong in this group."

It might have Marlene that brought us together, but it was really when Ash came in, that we finally developed our mission. Ash, or 'Incendiary,' was just starting high school when she joined The Neighborhood Watch.

We had made a name for ourselves as three already by exposing a perp who got off by poisoning dog biscuits: 'The Cookie Monster.'

Marlene made the prediction and told us where to go. As a beautiful man and woman, Gemini could pluck confessions out of just about anyone. As Gemini met The Cookie Monster on a date in the park, I laid in wait in the bushes. When The Cookie Monster ran, I leapt out and detained him. Actually, I kicked his living shit out, and then I sat on his throat and waited for the police.

The perp got off with two months in prison. He came back home and put a Christmas tree in his window. This is when Ash showed up.

Though the blackened evidence of a burned down house stood clearly only two blocks down from my own house, we could not believe Ash when she told us her powers. "A pyro without fire?" said Marlene, leaning into the light from her Tiffany lamp. "A burned down house without smoke?!"

Ash led us to the woods where an old half-collapsed house lay abandoned in weeds. Green and yellow climbers had pushed into every window and broken down every door. The roof looked like cardboard left in the rain. Ash creaked open the rusted old gate and Marlene, Gemini (the girl Gemini) and I followed her up the walkway toward the front door.

Gemini asked Ash what we were doing here. Marlene closed her eyes and tensed her arthritic hands like she was hearing a message in the wind. I walked the perimeter and peered in the windows. There were two wooden chairs. One was knocked over. Both were missing pieces. I came to the back window which had still a little glass left. There was something carved in paneling under the window. It looked like two names but was so covered in dirt or in dust. I reached to scrape it off. When my fingers made contact, it was like touching a stove. The house was turning black. I looked in the sky and, though the sun was setting, that didn't explain the seering pads of my fingers.

I ran around to the front. Gemini and Marlene were now staring at Ash. Ash, who had her hands on each side of the doorframe, was pushing against the house with all her might, like she was going to push it over. With how intensely she pushed, it looked almost like someone was behind her, trying to force her to go in.

The house blackened like an expiring orange. It was like a fire in time lapse. The paneling blazed white gray like wood in a campfire. The roof began crinkling like tinfoil. We stepped back. It was intensely hot. It was like a nightmare of being unable to scoot back from a fireplace. The house before our eyes burned down, but there was no smoke, there was no fire, there was no severe damage to the forest around it except for the pale yellowing of the branches nearby or above it.

Ash began to look woozy. She was not up as right as she had been. I ran to her and, as she swooned, fireman-carried her away from the house. My lungs had no reaction. The air felt totally clear. But the way the heat plummeted down on me, it was like crawling into a pottery oven.

Now, as we sat mourning the death of Marlene, in the living room of the small house Gemini had inherited, Ash stared into her hands, perhaps mesmerized by all she had done, perhaps seeing now all the fire and smoke which had never been there, which even now only she could see.

I didn't know how to start the meeting. Marlene always started the meetings. Marlene did nothing special to start the meetings, only began impulsively sharing some relatively unimportant event from her day. I tried to start the same way. "I-" I began, and then felt stunted, as Marlene had died only last night, and I, in my mind's eye, had no recourse for steering out of the bad news and into the good. I was stuck at "I." "I," I said again.

"I wish Marlene was here," I finally managed.

Gemini (the boy Gemini) nodded. They sat staring blankly at Marlene's armchair and the Tiffany lamp. The lamp sat there glowing like Marlene. It was, in the silence, like those many moments when Marlene would suddenly be silent, receiving some transmission from the future.

"Seven houses," Ash said.

It was true. Counting the first abandoned house in the woods she showed us and the two she'd done accidentally before she'd met us, Ash had been the cause of seven burned down houses.

I had a direct purpose now to speak and spoke easily. "Those houses were just. We had just cause," I said.

"Seven," Ash said. "Seven houses. Five for Marlene. And now Marlene-" She paused. She looked at Gemini, then at the Tiffany lamp.

The Neighborhood Watch   47

Gemini sat up in their chair. "It was right," they said. "We knew what those men would have done. We knew-"

"Marlene is dead," said Ash. She widened her eyes and opened her hands. She stared at me now. "Marlene is dead, Toni. Marlene is dead."

"Marlene is dead," I said. "And we've got to carry her on. She built this. She trusted us."

"Marlene," said Ash. "Marlene could read the future." Ash nodded up and down, reasoning to herself with the kind of burned out intensity I had seen years before in myself. "If Marlene knew she was gonna die," and Ash rashly indicated the Ritz crackers still tightly Saran wrapped. "She died. She is dead." Ash pointed at the kitchen behind us, which had a roast Marlene left cooking in a crockpot. "She didn't know."

"She didn't want to upset us," said Gemini.

Ash shook her head. "She didn't know shit," she said. "She didn't know.

"Hey," I said. "That's not fair."

The charred remains of our four target houses remained like big charred skeletons.

"Seven," said Ash. "And we don't really know why?"

"Bad men-" I began.

"We don't know that," Ash said. She pointed at me and herself. "We don't know jack shit. But they," she pointed at Gemini and the ether. "They told us what we needed to hear. And then I, I-" She curled like a bug and held her head in her hands. "Four deliberate attempts to hurt someone. And then what was next? What was tonight? Was tonight another hit? Did we have a new target tonight?"

"Marlene created The Neighborhood Watch," I said. "Marlene gave us all a place to do good."

Ash sniggered. "All you did was assault. I destroyed four men's homes."

"They were bad men," I said.

Gemini nodded.

I tried to make it as clear as possible. "You've done a lot of good in this neighborhood. You've stopped a lot of bad people."

Ash put her fingers at her temples and furrowed her brow. She was mocking Marlene, one of Marlene's frequent visions. She began shaking and speaking in a deep, breathless voice like a possessed woman in a seance. "*MAN ON BIRCH STREET. MAN. MID-THIRTIES. THIRD HOUSE ON BIRCH.*" She squeezed the fingers of her armchair. "*VICTIM. SARA WHITE.*" Then she let go of her armchair and slumped down in it like a teenager. "Fuck," she said. "It's horseshit." She went silent, and stared ahead like she was watching something else.

In the silence, I thought more about Marlene.

Many weeks would go by without any houses, until a week would come where the Tiffany lamp flickered and Marlene death-squeezed the arms of her chair. *MAN ON BIRCH STREET. MAN. MID-THIRTIES. BIRCH. THIRD HOUSE.* Her eyes would roll back in her head. She would foam at the mouth. And then we'd suit up, wait for nightfall, and sneak into our places.

Gemini, as a man or a woman, would get themselves invited into the bad man's house for a drink. Ash and I would wait outside the man's house in the bushes. Ash would just rub her hands together while we sat in the cold looking in the man's window. I would eat a little creatine, and sit with my bag and my rope. Any sign of danger, any word of go-ahead from Gemini, and we'd break the door down and get started.

It was my job to incapcitate the fucker physically and then stuff him in the bag. I wouldn't kick him, but I would roll him around a little bit and then sit on the bag, so there was no way he could get out. After the first couple times, it only took Ash

The Neighborhood Watch

ten minutes tops to burn the whole thing down to the ground. I'd whisper to the man in the bag: "You may not know who you were gonna hurt yet. But now you've got no chance of hurting anyone here. When I let you out, it's gonna be a whole new world. For you."

When I'd finally let the man out of the bag, it would still take him half a minute to orient himself to the right end, unc-inch it and crawl out. In that half-minute, all three of us would dive back into the bushes. And then we'd see it. A fireless, smokeless tragedy: a man seeing his own home. Maybe it was the house he'd grown up in. Maybe it was a house he'd swooped in and bought. Whatever the man's house had once meant to him, now it was a big heap of ash and black boards.

"The Neighborhood Watch," said Ash, who was so sullen now it was as if she had entirely given up hope. "There is never any Neighborhood Watch. 'The Neighborhood Watch' is an arbitrary sign on an arbitrary street corner. No one ever makes a neighborhood watch. It's a sign. It's a yellow sign jutting out of someone's juniper bushes. Who *really*, who really takes the Neighborhood Watch seriously besides children?"

"I do," I said. I was very proud of this. Ash met my eyes. "I believe in The Neighborhood Watch."

After moments of great tension, Gemini tied their hair back and started the meeting. "Tonight as The Neighborhood Watch, though as we admittedly carry on with no leader, we carry on with Duty, with Honor, with Justice. Anyone, who is to these terms opposed, must speak now, or hold their peace." Without checking Ash or me for reaction, they carried about, as Marlene always would, to peel the Saran wrap off the cheese and Ritz crackers, and then held the plate out to each remaining member of The Neighborhood Watch.

I took one.

Gemini took one.

And not without some great hesitation, Ash finally took one.

"We immediately report all suspicious activities," said Gemini, before taking her first bite of cracker. "For we are The Neighborhood Watch."

Ash and I also bit into our crackers. But I immediately frowned. There was something like a paper wrapper left in my cracker. I noticed the others frowned too. I held my cracker up to my eyes and stared at it. There was a small white corner under the cheese.

I lifted up the cheese. It was a small folded white paper. Without the weight of the cheese, it began to expand out of its fold. I took it and unfolded it completely. There was a small message inside.

Gemini read it out first: "*MAN ON QUEENS*. MAN. *MIDDLE FIFTIES*. VICTIM. *THE BUBBLEGUM BEACON*."

Requiem for a Radicalized Superman
by CJ Huntington

Superman you just threw a car through this gas station wall
And I'm just trying to get a small black coffee.
I don't even use the milk they make out of almonds anymore because
California doesn't have enough water for that.

It is *barely* 9 in the morning.

Superman we need good journalists,
And you're out here flying around
like that story is going to write itself.

You know I fell once
On the river shore when I was 19,
Right on down a hill and done
cracked my head right on open,
Woke up in an ambulance.

You know I'm still in debt from it?

Superman you've got super strength,
Right?
[Yes pardon me if that is presumptuous]
Well there's a problem at the penthouse, see—
yes, well, see, it's the money, see—
The money doesn't belong to them.
It does, in fact, belong to me.

And the oil execs,
At Exon and Shell—
well I mean
Superman, there's no heaven or hell!
And sure I know how to save the world—
Honest I do—
You can read about it,

in my zine.
Nah for real,
we have free copies at my mutual aid group.

Every hero's got a code,
and there by the grace of god go you.
But half my state burnt down last year,
and beating up muggers
just ain't gonna do!
I stitch up the boys' clothes,
and their hands when they get cut,
in exchange for discount produce
and pirated movies and what not.
[Yeah I also help fix their shitty old Hondas so keep your mouth shut]
Do you need a seamstress,
Superman,
or a nurse,
or a back-alley mechanic?
Maybe just keep you company,
give you some new ideas,
whisper in your ear
some of the things I've seen?
Have you ever heard of Bookchin,
Superman?
What about Nester Mahkno?
No—no, Superman, my friend,
don't worry about it.
Let's just try to be discreet.
We'll have plenty of time to discuss
on our way to Wall Street.

You're Almost a Super Hero, Dad

by Lynette G. Esposito

"Look what you have done, Daddy. Those people in the little houses can stay in their homes. My friend, Bill, lives there. He is the neatest guy. Can we go see him sometime?"

"We have to go to the hospital for your treatment today, Johnny. Maybe."

"Maybe what? They said I had weeks, maybe."

Arthur sighed. "So, you think I am a super hero?

"Bill told me some big money guy bought all the land here but you stopped him from tearing down all these houses. How did you do that, Dad? Only a superhero could do that."

Arthur sighed again only deeper this time. "I know the money guy."

"Yeah, but, Dad, it takes a lot of power to save so many people. Bill says he has no place to go. And nobody paid him anything. You saved my friend."

Arthur sucked in his breath. I am the money guy passed through his mind. I am no super hero. I am the villain. I just delayed the evictions until my son dies. There, I said it even though it is just a thought grinding in my mind. I am going to lose the only thing that makes my own life worth living. I should tell Johnny the truth but it is great having my son think I am a hero. "I didn't save your friend exactly,"

"But, Dad, you did something great. You gave them time."

Arthur felt like he had been struck in the face. He had given a few weeks to strangers but he couldn't do the same for Johnny.

"When I get to heaven, I am going to tell God what you did."

Arthur shivered. He had done a lot of things. "What are you talking about?"

"You being a super hero. If I grow up and I beat this thing I have, I want to be like you."

Arthur was thinking about this conversation with his son while kneeling before Johnny's casket. So many people had come to the funeral. His little boy, not yet ten, had made such an impact. I want to be just like you he whispered to the boy laying so still on the velvet pillow.

Arthur imagined Johnny laughing as if his father had made a joke. Two weeks ago, his raggedy blond son had been laughing.

Arthur lowered his head. A friend came, put his hand on his shoulder and led him away from the silver casket.

Days later, or maybe it was weeks or maybe it was months, Arthur didn't know. Time meant little to him now. Johnny's light had gone out and Arthur wasn't quite himself. He named his project Johnny's Haven and delayed the eviction notices for three years. Real estate goes up so he knew his investment wouldn't suffer. He didn't want to go against a boy who was going to talk to God about him. So, Arthur gave time.

He looked at the picture of his son on his desk. Written across the front on the bottom just above the bronze frame in a childish scrawl were the words *Marvel, One of a Kind*. Johnny had written that while getting his treatment and given it to Arthur for Father's Day.

Arthur had been staring at the picture for so long his eyes hurt. I wonder what my son would have been like if he had had the time to grow up. Arthur talked to himself.

He stood up from his expensive chrome chair. Arthur didn't want to waste another moment. He knew without thinking it, Johnny was with him, his son, the super hero, who had

Lynette G. Esposito

Hell is Empty and My Daughter Saves the Day

Kate Falvey

This day limps and whimpers
in a sudden mob of jeers and taunts.
Remorse muscles in, blocking
the tease of possible light
with a fuggy pulse of wayward,
gravel-blind, monstrous self-absorption.

This is the end of the world
and only imps and devils are afoot,
the wrecks beset by iron-hearted looters
stealing movement from the air, inviting
a tepid Armageddon, an inglorious
surrender to a dearth of visionary gleams.

And in she streams, flinging horrors
from the waste, a flick of her moonlight
cape, a toss of her earth-glow hair, seeds
glinting in the arc of her unwary arms,
falling from her breath in their own self-
fulfilling shimmer of death-defying rain.

The Chocolate Drop
by Aurora Lewis

Domonique sat looking at her tablet. There was so much crime she couldn't stop all of it, but she would try for damn sure with Uncle Vic's help. Picking up her gym bag, she pulled out her uniform and began to dress. It was nearly 10 PM. She worked overtime finishing a book she was assigned to edit by the publishing company where she worked. It was a book of experimentally unstructured poems that gave her a headache but was now gone.

After dressing, she looked at her reflection in the mirror; everything was perfect. Domonique was tall, slender, and shapely. Her complexion was rich dark brown, although she covered half of her face with a mask. She wore her hair natural, cascading below her shoulders. Her attire: a brown leotard, matching leggings, brown leather gloves, and her prize procession: a pair of kick-ass Nike SFB Gen, brown leather boots. Based on witness descriptions, the police gave her the moniker, The Chocolate Drop. Not only because of her attire, but also because she had a calling card, a single chocolate drop piece of candy left at every crime scene on the forehead of the criminals she apprehended. However, she was a Person of Interest; the authorities didn't want a vigilante patrolling the streets.

Domonique always wore an amber necklace given to her by her late Uncle Vic, which she carefully tucked inside her leotard. It was among the many gifts he gave her when she graduated from college. He told her amber contained electric energy, acting directly on the human energy system, and psychic circuitry. Her uncle also told her the stone soothes, calms, heals, and, most importantly, protects. Domonique had no idea what this meant or why Uncle Vic insisted she wear the necklace at all times, in time she learned why.

She went to the kitchen to retrieve her small brown backsling bag, filling it with a handful of chocolate drop candy and restraining ties. Everything about her secret persona, including the candy, was inspired by Uncle Vic. When she was a kid, he said she was as sweet as a chocolate drop and always had a few in his pocket when he came to visit. Uncle Vic was her mother's younger brother, only 18 months apart. He was a substitute father as her natural father walked out before she was born. Uncle Vic was the family's go-to guy, taking her to movies, amusement parks, and museums, giving her books, and sharing his wealth of knowledge. To say she loved him wasn't nearly enough. She revered him.

When Domonique was 22, Uncle Vic died from injuries from a carjacking. It was a few months after graduation. He was distinguishingly handsome, well dressed, and drove sporty luxury cars, which made him a target on the violent streets. His death was a devastating blow to Dominque and her mother. Dominique vowed to avenge him and prevent other innocent people from having the same fate that took Uncle Vic from her. She started training in martial arts before she was in her teens, something Uncle Vic insisted upon and promoted, paying for all of her training. I have plans for you, he told her, now calling her 'Drop.' By the time she was 20, she was a master in Mixed Martial Arts; Judo, Muay Thai, Brazilian Jiu-Jitsu, Boxing, Karate, Kickboxing, and Wrestling. This was something she didn't share with her friends or co-workers; even her mother didn't know how advanced she had become. Perhaps she was predetermined to live this secret dual life? Although Uncle Vic was no longer alive, he would come to her, not in dreams, but his spirit appeared when her help was needed in those mean streets. This was another secret she didn't share with her mother.

As she walked out down the stairwell of her apartment building, there was Uncle Vic.

"What took so long, Drop?" he asked, "Someone needs you over on 8th."

"I'm on my way, Uncle Vic," she answered without hesitating, running down the steps, and out the rear-entry door. Uncle Vic was still beside her.

"There are two of them in a dark blue van trying to snatch a girl on her way home from the library."

"I got it, Uncle Vic."

Domonique ran faster than a cheetah in the direction Uncle Vic pointed. She was there in seconds and saw two men dragging a girl about 15 into a van. They didn't even see Domonique coming when she rose from the ground and drop kicked both in the face with her Nike boots. They were knocked out cold. The girl looked on in astonishment as she wiped tears from her eyes.

"Who are you, where did you come from, how did you do that?" the girl asked, her words running together, looking from the two kidnappers, then back to Domonique.

"You shouldn't be out this late, let me get you home," Domonique responded without answering the girl's questions. "What are you doing out so late by yourself?"

"My brother was supposed to pick me up, but he didn't show when the library closed. I thought I'd be ok. I just live a couple blocks away," the girl said, still sniffing from her tears.

Domonique pulled a cellphone from one of the assailant's jacket pockets, both were still out cold. Tying their hands and feet together with zip ties, she rolled them over on their backs. She placed a chocolate candy drop on each of their foreheads, took a photo, and sent it to the nearest precinct. She then took the girl under her arm and was off running. Her name was Sheila, and Domonique had her home in front of her building in less than a minute. Sheila was bewildered and couldn't grasp what took place in the last few minutes and the swiftness of Domonique's running feet.

"Are you from Wakanda? Some kind of superhero?" Sheila asked Domonique. She was serious.

"No, I'm not," Domonique responded, slightly grinning. She did have powers that she attributed to the necklace Uncle Vic gave her. "Get yourself in your apartment, and don't let me catch you at night on the streets alone again. Do I need to speak to your parents or that brother of yours?"

Sheila shook her head, indicating she understood that nothing like this would happen again. Stopping short of closing the door to her building, she looked into Domonique's eyes. "I forgot to say thank you, what's your name?"

"They call me The Chocolate Drop," she said as she took off.

Domonique heard Uncle Vic's voice: "Good Work, Drop."

"What's next, Uncle Vic?"

"Brighton, over by King, gay kid is about to get the crap beat out of him."

Domonique and Uncle Vic were there just in time. A young man was shoved against the flower shop wall. Another guy was holding a knife to his throat while three other thugs were egging him on.

"Cut the faggot. Chop off his pecker. We don't allow no stinking queers!" they shouted.

An old woman was sitting at a bus stop avoiding making eye contact with the thugs, but she saw Domonique moving faster than lightning in their direction. Her body was turning like a whirling dervish, her booted feet flying in a circular motion knocking the three hog-calling thugs to the ground. They were out like a light.

Turning her attention to the knife welding goon, Domonique drop-kicked him in his ass with so much force, air blew from his mouth, causing him to slam to the concrete. Leaning over him, she bitch-slapped him so hard his eyes blinked, and he was out like the other three. It all happened so fast, the guy being attacked didn't have enough time to move, and the old lady on the bus stop bench sat there with her mouth open. Domonique took some of the restraining ties in her bag and tied the 4 creeps together in a row, and placed a chocolate drop on each of their foreheads. She told the young man standing by to call the cops and asked the old woman if she could stay and report as a witness. The two agreed as they watched her disappear into the night.

When the cops arrived, a news-van joined them. "Looks like The Chocolate Drop has been here," a police officer called out as he placed the candy in an evidence bag. The thugs were coming to, but were still in a daze. The young man and old lady gave their witness accounts and were interviewed live for a local news channel. The Chocolate Drop was becoming famous, and the authorities were worried something terrible would soon happen to her. This was her tenth rescue in as many days.

When Domonique got home, she was alone, Uncle Vic always left her after their work was done. She threw her clothes in the small stackable washer in her utility closet, wiped off her boots, took a shower, and went to bed. Domonique still had three books sitting on her desk at work that needed editing. She wanted to get an early start, she was finished with the poetry book, and now a memoir and fiction novel were left. Domonique's degree was in liberal arts, as an avid reader of several genres; fiction, non-fiction, technical, and the arts, hoping one-day to have her own publishing company. Crawling into bed, she turned off the light and went right to sleep.

The next day at work, the talk was all about The Chocolate Drop news accounts from television, newspapers, and social media news outlets. No one would ever suspect that the brown-skinned heroine was Domonique as she always wore her hair in a tight bun, with wire-framed glasses, and slightly oversized clothes. There was only a hint of her beauty beneath her façade and none of her strength and power. It was going to be a long day, but she liked her job and the people she worked with who considered her a little odd. She'd go on breaks or lunches with her co-workers, but never socialized with them after hours. On weekends during the day, she'd visit her mother, treating her to lunch and a movie, always returning home as soon as it got dark. Everyone thought she had a secret lover; this only made her chuckle at her denials.

That night, Uncle Vic was waiting for her in the stairwell

of her apartment.

"Liquor store over on Broadway," he told her, winking

"Let's go!" she said, smiling as she raced down the steps and out the door. "How many?"

"Does it matter?" he asked

"Nope, not really."

Damien Strong
by Vincent A. Alascia

I watched the groupie dress. The cool light slipping in the tour bus window ignited her magenta hair in a halo of color. I watched the dark line of her jeans slide over the curve of her hips to just above the line of her skimpy thong and thought about asking her to come back to bed. I shook my head, and the thought ran away into the night. She pulled on her shirt, grabbed her jacket, and blew me a kiss before heading to the exit at the front of the bus. I always like it when they leave on their own. I avoid the uncomfortableness of asking them.

I waited a bit as she talked to one of the roadies and then heard her get in a car. I left the bed and dressed. I needed some fresh air. I spotted a piece of paper with a phone number scrawled on it, that my guest left behind. I was about to crumble it up and changed my mind. Folding it in half I slipped it in the front pocket of my jeans. I never wanted to be *that* rockstar, but here I was, groupies in every city. Sex and nothing but sex, I was a user, but hey we all can't be saints.

Outside, I spotted the bus driver. "We gonna be here a little longer?"

"At least another hour, the speaker towers are being a pain in the ass again."

I nodded. "I'm going to take a walk around the block, clear my head, you know. Don't leave without me."

"What and have your dragon lady manager bite my head off?"

He was right. Michele was not one to fool with. I wouldn't be surprised if she wasn't back on the stage wrestling the speaker towers back in their road cases herself.

The block around the civic center was deserted by now.

The air had a coolness to it as the concrete around me gave off the august heat from the day. I turned a corner by a closed and boarded up sandwich shop with some apartments on top of it when I heard something soft, but unmissable. Crying. I looked around. Alone down here. I strained my ears and could hear the sound coming from the rooftop, some eight stories above me. Now I know I should have just kept on walking, but something about this pulled at me. To the right of the building was an alley. I went into it and looked for a way up. Fire escapes hung about ten feet from where I stood. I took one more look around and confident no one could see, I leaped. A little too much as I wound up on the third landing. Climbing over the rail I hurried up the iron stairs making as little sound as I could.

A woman with black hair in a denim jacket and torn jeans sat on the edge of the roof sobbing into the street below. I slowly approached.

"Damn it Becca, I hear you."

I stopped.

The girl shifted around to look at me. "Who the Hell…" She stopped and I could tell from her eyes she was asking herself what the hell is Damien Strong doing on a rooftop with her. "How did you get up here?"

"You wouldn't believe me if I told you. I was taking a walk while they loaded up the truck and I heard someone crying."

She looked over the edge at the street. "You heard me from down there?"

I pointed out the right side of my head. "Good ears."

"Just go back to your tour bus or whatever and leave me alone."

"You sure? I thought you could use someone to talk to. It looks like you might be planning to do something kind of drastic."

"Drastic, the story of my life. You don't know anything. It's all turned to shit, talking ain't going to fix it. Nothing will." She leaned towards the open air and let gravity take her. The air rushing from her lungs barely left room for a scream.

Without even a thought I leapt over the ledge after her. I managed to grab onto her at about the fifth floor. I landed feet first with her in my arms. My legs buckled and we tumbled to the sidewalk. The girl scrambled off me and puked in a storm drain. I unfolded my legs and heard the shin bones snap back into place. I gave them a minute as they healed. I stood up and went over to help the girl up from the curb.

She looked at me and then up at the roof. "How? You?" She shook. "What the fuck?" And then punched me in the chest. "*Really*, you couldn't just let me do it?"

"No. I couldn't just stand there and watch someone throw a life away."

"Oh, spare me all the life is precious bullshit. What do you know?"

I grabbed her arm and turned it over to expose the needle marks and bruises I caught a glimpse of on the way down. "I know what these are. I'm not going to lie to you. Getting high is a lot of fun but it has its cost. You might think throwing yourself off the rooftop pays them but all it does is push it off on someone else. Believe it or not there is someone out there whose world would come to an end without you in it."

"She threw me out," the girl said, and beyond the puffy eyes and shaking lips I could see my words had hit something.

"You gotta fix your own messes. Decide who do you love more: that needle or your partner? It's not like there's superheroes running around to do it for you." I winked at her, and she cracked a faint smile. "Go home, you got a second chance to make it count for something."

"Thank you," she whispered.

I turned and walked away with a bit of a limp but that should be gone by morning. I'm not fully used to my powers but for the first time I think I've done some good. I made it back to my tour bus as the guys had just finished. It was fifteen hours to the next city, and the show goes on.

Annie Rescues Herself
by Kate Falvey

She struggles to breathe in the icy air,
gulping trouble and guile from voices
not her own.

She has learned to skate between
dazzlers and blunderers on the gridlocked
city rink,

ankles burning with intent and
tentative discovery of the sweet
spot for

equipoise, remaining mostly upright,
steering into a valiant glide, knowing
a fall

is imminent, inescapable
when risking the thrill of
the ride.

Everything I learned in life I learned twice

by Alex Werner

When Spiderman taught me
With great power comes
Great responsibility
I walked out shirked mine
Dropped the ball
When Batman taught me
I'm only smiling on the outside
You might join me for a weep
I smiled and was invulnerable
Until I learned the difference between
Smiling and showing my teeth
When Superman taught me
Villains are made not born
I trusted strangers who
Offered candy or love
I cannot say how large is
The number of times I've
Made and been made a villain
When Doctor Strange taught me
No matter the danger I must go
I shut my eyes and ran through
I found myself lost
I cannot learn from mistakes
Not those of others not even my own
So, everything I learned in life
I learned twice

How Joe "The Nose" Mulligan Survived 2020
by Jen Mierisch

The man with the big nose fidgeted on the plush office chair.

"I've never done anything like this before, Doc," he said. "I mean, I'm a superhero, for Christ's sake."

"There's no shame in seeking counseling, Joe," replied Dr. Baird. "Tell me what's on your mind."

"I just feel so… useless, ya know? Without my sense of smell, I'm nothing. I mean, I'm Joe 'The Nose' Mulligan!"

"Of course. I'm familiar with your work."

"I can smell a bomb while it's still being made. I can smell a drug shipment a hundred miles out to sea. I can smell a lying suspect three buildings over!" His face fell. "I could, anyway. Before."

"Understood. I'm sure it's been a difficult adjustment. Has your employer given you a leave of absence?"

"Yeah," he sighed. "The FBI's cool. Government job, good benefits. But there I am, sitting at home, while my wife leaves for work. I got nothing to do. I'm going crazy. Please tell me it isn't permanent."

"Inconclusive," said Dr. Baird. "Most COVID-19 patients regain their sense of smell after two to eight weeks. Others still have sensory loss months after recovery." She opened a file folder. "How long since you lost yours?"

"Three weeks, Doc. My wife Amy even made my favorite food the other day, these scalloped potatoes that only she makes. It's, like, a thing for us. She fixes those potatoes when she knows I'm coming home from an assignment. I smell them when I leave the airport, and I know she's looking forward to seeing me, ya know? And nothing. Couldn't smell a thing. How'd I catch this goddamn virus anyway?"

"Well, you may be superhuman, but you're still human, Joe."

"What if I never get it back?" He stood and started pacing the room.

"Odds are excellent that you will regain your sense of smell. Still, you might want to prepare yourself for the possibility that it won't be as powerful as before," Dr. Baird said gently.

"What'll I do? I'll be out of a job!"

"Do you have other talents, interests?"

"Nothing I'm real good at."

"As a child, what did you aspire to be?"

He shrugged. "A veterinarian. Loved animals. Too dumb for vet school."

"Listen, Joe, these feelings of anger, loss, anxiety, they're all very normal. You might benefit from joining a support group, like Abscent."

"Support group?" He scoffed. "Not really my thing, Doc."

"Well, please come back and see me next week, and we'll talk some more."

#

"How's it going today, Joe?"

"Meh."

"Are you feeling all right? You seem to have lost weight."

He shrugged. "No sense of smell. Can't taste anything. Why eat."

"Keep at it, Joe. And keep applying that steroid nasal spray. Sometimes smell will return a little bit at a time. Have you been able to get out and enjoy this weather?"

He looked up with sunken eyes. "Nah. I don't even want to leave the house, Doc. I feel like I'm blind or something. Normally I could smell if there was something wrong with the car, or if there was a gas leak someplace. If we went for takeout, I knew how clean their kitchen was. I could even smell if other people had the flu, so I knew who to avoid. Now, I got nothing. Hell, I can't even tell if I have B.O."

"You're fine on that front, Joe. You went to an acupuncturist, yes?"

He chuckled humorlessly. "Heh. Bunch of needles in my back, and bupkis."

"There is evidence that the brain adjusts to compensate for the loss of one sense. So even if you end up with long-term sensory loss, you may find your other senses become more keen."

Joe sat up straighter. "You mean I might get super hearing or vision, instead of super smell?"

"Usually the process takes about a year."

"Oh."

"Tell me about your week. How have you been spending your time?"

Joe shrugged. "Watched TV, walked my dogs. Tried to help Amy out, fixed stuff around the house. Folks at work sent me a get-well card, that was nice."

"Anything else?"

"Oh, I turned forty last weekend. Friends threw me a little surprise party, in the backyard, masks on, ya know. Amy baked the cake. She sent me out to the store, and everybody was waiting when I got back."

"That's nice. I imagine, with your particular talents, you don't get surprised very often."

He scratched the stubble on his chin. "You know, you're right, Doc. I would've smelled that cake a mile away. It was kinda nice to be surprised."

"So then, it's not all bad."

"Well, mostly bad."

Dr. Baird peered over her glasses.

"But not all bad, Doc."

#

"You look happy today, Joe."

The grinning patient took a seat.

"The Nose is back, Doc!"

"That's wonderful news. Has your olfactory function completely returned?"

"About 75 percent. Which puts me at about 500 times the normal human sense of smell. So…"

"Still super?"

"Still super!"

"And you're back to work?"

"Yep. Well, ya know, the boss still wants me to take it easy for a while. So, get this, guess what they got me doing over there?"

"What's that?"

"Helping out the CDC. Turns out they can train dogs to sniff out viral infections. Of course, now that I know what COVID smells like, I can detect it way faster than any lab. You're looking at the head animal trainer for the new K-9 unit."

"That's terrific, Joe."

"Hey listen, Doc, even though I don't need you anymore, I guess, I wanted to say thanks. It was good to come here all those times and talk things out."

"That's what I do. I'm glad I was able to help, Joe."

"I thought counseling was for wimps, no offense. But now I realize it's just talking. I like talking."

"I'm here to listen. Come back any time."

"I will."

At the door, he paused, chuckling.

"Hey, Doc?"

"Yes?"

"Smell ya later."

I'm a superstar, and super high, but superhero?

by Timothy Arliss OBrien

~~~Where is my hero?~~~

Nothing is worse than when there isn't a hero to rush in and fix everything.

Me: cast as the damsel in distress
Scene: a tragic distressing event
where I need rescuing.

The Knight in Shining Armor: missing.

Refusing to show up for work,
skies full of beacons and distress symbols.
Missing in action, and nowhere to be found.

I hope I'm not being too redundant here but I don't know how else to ask for help.

Do I take out a help wanted ad in the paper?
Do I write a strongly worded email to my elected officials?
Maybe all the heroes have heard there is a war on and they are fighting to upkeep democracy and freedom.

You know it's so terrible.
My favorite strip club moved to a new venue and there isn't a good view of the sausages from every seat in the house like there used to be, and I'm almost out of joints to smoke.
I wish someone could save me.

~~~Am I the superhero?~~~

It's true:

I'm supposed to save the world.

But I don't know if I can.

I don't even think I believe in superheroes.

No one has ever been there for me
when I've needed rescuing.

And holy fuck have I needed to be rescued before.

One time a tindr date went wrong,
and I was too stoned to find the front door.
So I had to exist in misery for almost six hours.

Another time, a tornado was impending and bigger than I had
ever seen, and guess who was right in the direct path?
Me and my kitten.

Then there was a time I realized I was in a cult,
after I had cut off all my family and friends,
and I had no clue who to ask for help.

Maybe it's time I call myself,
lift the boulder off me,
and on my cape,
And fly me an escape,
to freedom: to better waters:
Utopia and paradise.

A one-way ticket maybe only I can give myself.
Try it with me.
Let's be rescuers.
Let's be rescued.

Unbreakable
by Phyllis Hemann

The bullets you lob
at me bounce
off my field of impenetrability.

Day by day

the layers of fat
under my skin
become my armor,
necessary
to protect me
from a world
inspired with hate
for anything other —
odd, weird, different unusual —
not dimensional
enough to fit into
an overhead bin inside
the forehead. Their punches
bounce off

my body armor absorbing
the impact, wiggling, reverberating
inside.

My Mother, a Bionic
by Anna Laura Falvey

My mother worries one
bone in her body like the wind
warps a grain field. It is the glowing
metal rod in her left shin -- the poetry

dowsing rod. At night she sleeps still
and the rod points up to her blood-
pumping heart, twice out, years long
to work, still -- and glows blue slant

into her poetry, weighing her heart
with dull, floating blue chrome,
brightening her eyes with song and,
yes, more life.

The Powers of Outer Space
by E.T. Starmann

Long ago (350 million years ago, but who is counting?), there was a grave distress signal sent from a dying star, a star so endlessly far it could only be energy from that initial universal explosion, that big, big Big Bang, and, as far as our organization has observed, is breaking right about now through the milk of the Milky Way Galaxy.

The strange rays of this strange communication have split and are breaking in as would a meteorite splitting in sporadic strikes down to earth.

Our organization has observed various results as split pieces collide in various situations on earth. The results of some combinations have exhibited as follows:

EXHIBIT A: One Harold A. Eric of Des Moines, Iowa on Friday, at 7:30pm. Alias: THE GREEN MAN

Harold was sitting on a green plastic chair on his back deck when he stood up at once and exclaimed.

He had been trying to, as the woman on channel thirteen had suggested he ought, "Seize the appropriate opportunity by adopting the appropriate attitude, and make the poor rabbit explode." He acquired the appropriate concentration to his mind, his forehead reddening, his eyebrows arching, arching, arching–

He did not see the stone fall from the sky, but sensed it in the top of his eyes as one would an eyelash.

It was only as loud as a car crash an intersection away–a kick of dust so fast and sudden a small cloud bloomed from the ground.

Harold spilled his lemonade and kicked over his beer. His

chair fell backwards without him.

It is strange how an animal always predicts each disaster. Moments before impact the rabbit had run straight for the explosion.

"Bucky?" Harold had said, as he inched toward the plume of red dust.

(The rabbit he had both christened condemned to combust.)

"Give a name to your object," the channel-thirteen woman had said. "Repeat so that your mind may listen. Only then may you explode something with your mind." A smart woman, the woman from channel thirteen, thought Harold.

The red plume of dust was now just a pale imitation, like the ghost of a tree, seeing itself in a puddle and drifting away out of fright. Bucky was nowhere to be found. Harold held his forearm above his eyes and walked into the haze of the dust.

Harold came to the crater and tapped its edge with his toe. The small crater was about the size and shape of a cheap satellite dish. Inside it was a small piece of glass.

"Mirror, mirror," said Harold. He coughed in one hand and compulsively jingled the keys in his pocket with the other.

"Well," he said, and picked up the mirror. It was not a flat mirror but a silvery stone and only its topside was flat and reflective. He removed his hat and scratched the hairs of his forehead with the same idle fingers and brim. Would he look into it or would it look into him? HAHAHA!

Something about his own reflection in this small piece of glass made him nervous. He wiped his mouth because a feeling like hunger had filled it with spit.

"Where on earth did you come from?" Harold said to the silvery stone. He tossed it up and down in his hand. He looked into the sky.

He looked at the stone. Two black eyes he didn't know grinned up at Harold. He dropped the stone and it tumbled away. He tripped in the crater and fell. Harold looked in every direction, but there was no one around. The stone, like a thing so much larger than he was, sat staring him down.

After a heavy night's sleep, Harold climbed into his truck.

He had put the stone in a box and set it beside him in the passenger seat. "Put your destiny into your hands," the channel-thirteen woman had said. He was going back to the channel-thirteen woman. He had to explain to her that Bucky had run away in the wind.

Harold pulled into the parking lot where the channel-thirteen woman's sons sold rabbits. As he pulled in between the two white lines which would hold his truck, he adjusted his rearview mirror. He saw the black eyes once more and drove over the curb.

Harold took the silvery stone from the box and slipped it in his pocket. A bell above the door chimed as he entered. The channel-thirteen woman was still not around. Again, it was only her youngest son, Ranger, whom Harold had known as a boy. Ranger was picking flies from an electrical lamp when he looked up at Harold.

A general principle he had learned throughout life, Harold did not make eye contact with Ranger.

"The rabbit–," Harold said.

"Well, well," said Ranger. "If it isn't Harold Eric Ericson." (If it wasn't "Harold Eric Ericson" it was "Old Eric Harold Harrison.")

"The rabbit," said Harold.

"The rabbit?" said Ranger.

"Well, a rabbit. I need a new rabbit," said Harold. Harold had replaced the habit of jingling keys in his pocket with worrying the stone.

"Hey, come here," said Ranger. "Let me get a look at you."

There was the sound of another person coming in through the shadowy door behind the counter. "Hey Darrelson!" Ranger said over his shoulder. "Come on out here. Old Eric Harold Haroldson has returned."

"To return is to come back into oneself more fully and to do again what one once intended with now more will than before," the channel-thirteen woman had said.

Darrelson stepped out from the shadowy door. He was like a man made of clay molded over a boiler. He emerged from the shadowy door as do shadows cast from a locomotive exiting the tunnel. "Harold," he said. He held his hand out to Harold. Darrelson's hand had a distinct look to it, like it always had just done with strangling a bird. "Nice to see you."

"Nice to see you too," said Harold, who did not make eye contact with Darrelson either.

Darold had been a chump in high school. Ranger reminded him: "Do you remember, Darrelson, when Harold lost his pants and ran through the cafeteria looking for help?"

Darrelson smiled and filled the room with a thoughtful light air. "I do," said Darrelson. "I do."

"And do you remember," said Ranger, "when Harold was voted most likely to succeed?"

"I do," he said. "I do." Darrelson grimaced and tightened two fists.

Ranger slowly made his way behind Harold as if he were a dangerous gunman. "You sure you want to risk another rabbit?" he said.

The channel-thirteen woman had said also that, "To be one's self was to never lose sight of one's self, even when trapped in the eyes of the other. To do anything with any reality was to do it with certainty."

"I am certain that I am here to buy one more rabbit," said Harrold with certainty.

Ranger shoved his hands under Harold's pits. Harold's arms hung there like a dog's. He had held onto his stone so now the two brothers saw it as it came out of his pocket.

Ranger spoke first. "What the hell is that?" he said.

And then they two popped like balloons.

Harold had "seized the appropriate opportunity by adopting the appropriate attitude" with perhaps a bit more certainty than even before.

Ranger and Darrelson were now two side-by-side piles of what Harold remembered as 'gak' from his elementary school science fair project.

Harold stepped over Ranger and Darrelson and made his way behind the counter for a rabbit. There was only one rabbit. It was white and as fluffy as a basketball, with a little brown tuft on its head shaped like a heart. Its cute black-button eyes stared up at Harold. "I will name you Buckman," he said. "But I will never have an explosive attitude in my exchanges with you for I have suffered too much losing, losing–" But he could not bring himself to say 'Bucky.'

As Harold walked forward away from his solution to his two earlier problems, Darrelson and Ranger by name, he granted that this was indeed the power he had all along been praying for, the power he could share with almost anyone in the world.

Harold pulled a green Lone Ranger mask with sparkly stickers from a carousel stand by the exit of The Rabbits of Ranger and tied it over his eyes.

With his rabbit in one hand and his mirror in the other, Harold bid the two piles adieu: "I am not 'Old Eric Harold Haroldson' or 'Harold Eric Ericson.' Nor even am I 'Harold A. Eric.' No." He paused and held his masked head high. "I am the Green Man. Evildoers beware. Everybody look out. The Green

Man. I am The Green Man."

Harold left The Rabbits of Ranger and again the bell chimed above him.

Evildoers beware. Everybody look out. When you see the Green Man, just remember to shout.

EXHIBIT B: One Kaydell Bradshaw of Salt Lake City, Utah three Thursdays ago, at around 10:30pm. Alias: THE NIGHT LIGHT

The Night Light took on the characteristics of the moon after discovering a strange glowing/growing rock in his backyard. For the full story, listen to the DO Fiction Podcast's special two part series: "Masks!"

What would I change in the world if I could?
by Karla Linn Merrifield

You mean, what if I were Wonder Woman?
"The Spirit of Truth" with an arsenal of advanced technology,
butt-thigh-leg-arm muscles trained for combat, and golden
lasso to slay the idiot in the White House and cure the man in
E716?

Some nutcases think I'm some kind of Circe, witchy doctor-goddess,
renowned for my vast knowledge of magic potions and herbs.
I am neither. I can no more transform America's enemies within
into moral mortals than I can reverse my gentle husband's dementia.

The Little Villain That Could (But Could Only Do Good)
by Eric Thralby

How much good *would* the little villain that could?

Some say he would that he could. Others, that he would not wish any good.

But all little villains would be good if they could.

"But I am not good!" said he to the sky.

The sky looked around for the voice. When it saw the little villain, it came down and said, "I bet you would if you could."

"Not on your life!" said the little villain that could.

"You're only bad on the outside; you must be good on the in."

But the little villain ran away from the sky for he had so much evil he hoped he could do. He held that evil inside like gold close to his chest. The sky would take the evil away, and scatter it in the wind. That was sure. The little villain's eyes turned red with fear.

"I will go to the deepest, darkest place on the earth. And there I will build my dark lair of doom."

He climbed down into the deepest of pits. "I will kill them and crush them and take all their hope," the little villain sang to himself as he climbed down the long rope.

But, "What music is this?" said awaking sound sleepers. They rubbed the sleep from their eyes and gathered round the deep pit. "A voice of bright gold," they said as they gathered in rings. They lowered a basket and bade the little villain crawl in. But the little villain filled it with evil so when they reeled it back up they were cursed.

"I hope you all die for generations or worse," said the little villain.

They pulled up the basket and found it overspilling with gold.

"Huzzah!" the villagers said. And they ran down the hill screaming of how they would never go hungry again.

Come nightfall, the moon filled the dark pit with an eerie white light. "I will have a word with the moon," said the villain. The moon came close so the tides churned at the edge of the pit and threatened to spill. "No matter where I go," he said to the moon, "I cannot be myself."

"Well why don't you lie and try to be somebody else?" said the moon.

"I will burn cities and play in the ash," said the dastardly villain.

"I bet you would if you could," said the moon.

"I can. And I will!"

"OK," said the moon. "Go do it. I'll watch."

The tides rushed into the pit and raised the villain up and out like a flea from a spout.

"Go to the volcano and ask," said the moon to the villain.

So the little villain that could, killing each ant that he could, stomped his way up the side of the mountain of fire.

He came to the edge and spoke to the volcano: "I would have the earth suffer! I would have them all beg! From every throat will seer the word 'mercy!' And I will smile so wide because, of mercy, I will grant them none."

Hot red lava bubbled up at the small villain's toes. The volcano spoke like it was the center of earth: "Would you never do good?"

"Never ever do good."

"And what if you could?"

"Nope. No. Not a chance."

"Would you be my friend then?"

The little villain that could did not know what to say.

"You don't have to be my friend. You don't have to. But this is for you."

The volcano gave him a nice looking rock. It was porous and black. It was shaped like a starfish.

"Think about it, OK?" said the volcano.

The little villain that could picked up the rock. The way the rock fit in his fingers, it was like holding a hand in his own.

The little villain that could still was uncertain what he should say, so instead he just nodded.

"I will see you another time then," said the volcano.

The little villain that could held the black starfish and ran down the slope. What would he do now? *What would he do now?*

The little villain that could fell to his knees and cried into a hole.

unrescuable
by Lance Manion

Even superheroes get old. It seems obvious but not many people think about it. These individuals seem so super that the idea that they eventually need to be cared for just doesn't seem to register with most people. And on top of that, you can't just throw them in with normal folks at a nursing home.

Have you ever considered what could happen when you have a dementia patient that can lift twenty tons over his head?

It could be a formula for disaster.

So we take care of them here: a nursing home for superheroes.

You would think that dealing with what seems like an endless number of elderly supervillains trying one last time to vanquish an old foe would be the hardest part of the job, but it isn't. As loud and destructive as they can be.

Nor is the aforementioned dementia patient who is super strong and easily startled, although I can't express how careful you must be around him. Nobody wants a repeat of the 'Dropped Tapioca Incident.'

Trying to corral a bunch of old people for dinner, most of whom can fly or run at incredible speeds, or convincing a short-tempered woman who can shoot lasers out of her eyes to take her medications are also daunting tasks, but they are still not the most difficult part of my job.

The most difficult part?

That's easy.

When some of their super friends come for a visit.

You see, not all super heroes age at the same speed. We get

visitors who were born before there were even airplanes and telephones, and yet they look like they are in their thirties. Not a grey hair on their heads. And these super people love nothing more than to stop by unannounced to visit their old comrades and swap war stories about how they saved the world against tremendous odds or prevented some terrible incident from happening.

The thing is, then they leave. They leave and go back to saving the world and preventing terrible things from happening.

Our residents go back to sitting in their chairs or watching TV. Or, in the case of Telescopic Vision Man, watching satellites and space debris float around.

Imagine how hard that would be for a geriatric super hero. I've seen it firsthand and it's rough. One of our heroes has invisibility as one of his powers and it was weeks until we saw him again. Other than the sound of the occasional toilet flushing, it was like he wasn't even there.

Most of our residents spent their entire crime-fighting careers wearing a mask, and it's only after they have hung up their capes and tights that they truly realize that anonymity wasn't the only reason they wore them. Many of them dig them up for these visits so that their younger-looking friends can't see the pain etched on their faces. Pain or confusion or nothing at all. I think nothing at all being etched on your face must be the worst.

Must be hard to transition from super to old. Going from being punched through concrete walls and shaking it off to worrying about slipping in the shower and breaking a hip.

When a hero discovers his or her powers and wrestles with the responsibilities that come with them, the last thing they usually fear is aging. They would classify that, given the high mortality rates involved in crime-fighting, as a good problem to have. But then they do the last thing that anyone expects; they live through bullets and bombs. They survive death rays and mutant monsters, explosions and deadly poisons. Great loves and greater betrayals.

And they find themselves getting older.

And then old.

And then at our facility.

Cared for by super-ordinary people like myself.

Jodi Picoult once observed that "Superheroes were born in the minds of people desperate to be rescued." Nobody ever bothered to ask who rescues them.

Especially from the unrescuable.

The aging process is not gradual or gentle. It rushes up, pushes you over, and runs off laughing.
No one should grow old who isn't ready to appear ridiculous.

-John Mortimer

A Public Service Announcement On Behalf of All Your Heroic Friends:
by Nicholas Yandell

All your heroes will fail you

No matter how super they are.

Tremendous strength

Endurance and speed

Lapping the limits

Of human capacity

Decisively shattering

Known possibilities

May not be all

It's cracked up to be.

If great power comes

With great responsibility

Are you sure your heroes

Are up to the task?

It's exceedingly stressful

Dwelling in the shadow

Of presumed perfection

On the edge of a knife

In that arduous role

Of what you require from them.

All your heroes have weaknesses

Whether you deny it or not

Agonizing in anxiety

Increasingly strained

Inevitably exposing their inability

To become what you've decided they are.

In a realm

Of continuous mounting unreasonable demands

Who even needs Kryptonite?

Falling apart
Under duress

Life-altering decisions

In split-second durations

The lingering regret

Of every botched attempt.

All your heroes will burn out.

Like supernovas and falling stars

Succumbing to exhaustion

And escalating frustration,

Always just one step away,

From becoming your villain.

When filters lapse and words spill out

Or absent-minded actions

Falling outside the presence

Of your lofty expectations

Who will actually survive

The inferno of your disappointment?

Desperation can lead

To sinister possibilities

Bitterness has power too

At least for awhile

Devouring anger's energy

With no satiation

Empty and shriveling up

From lack of love and sustenance.

Nicholas Yandell

All your heroes have failed you

Will fail you

Are failing you now

Whether you know it or not

Or don't want to hear it

Or don't believe it.

Your heroes will always fall short

So maybe give them a break.

We're all living
Complicated missions

To this planet

To its people.

Heroes and villains

And all those under

That graphic blue sky

We long for acceptance

Strive to be valued

Including those up there

Tired of their towers

Longing to be seen

As simply human again.

Superman
by Gale Acuff

I stretch for the comic book at the top
of the spinner rack but I can't reach it
--I'm too small and my heroes are too high.
I don't think about what that means then but,
forty-three years later, it all makes sense
and would make a good comic book, too, if
I could pencil and ink and color and
letter. I still can't do any of these
but sometimes I write stories, even if
they are inside poems. If this is one. I
don't know--and I have a PhD in
literature and creative writing.

It was *Justice League of America*
--you get more heroes for your money and
they're good by themselves but work together
even better here. I'm a little boy
from the rural side of Marietta,
Georgia, which is countrified anyway.
I get into town only once a month
when my parents show they've kissed and made up
by taking me with them to eat out at
the Davis Brothers Cafeteria
where we slow-mo sideways-move through the line.
But I can't have spaghetti and French fries
together--Father won't let me. It's not
done, he says. Why, I ask. *Well, it's just not*,
he says. But why, I ask. *Because I said
so*, he says. Oh, I say. I get it now.

After supper I get my allowance
--twenty-five cents--and go to the drug store
to buy two comic books (twelve cents each and
a penny for Georgia sales tax--four cents
on the dollar: it's 1965).
Or one comic book and two candy bars
and two pieces of bubblegum. I can't

blow it yet but I'll get the hang of it,
like tying shoes or always zipping-up
when I get dressed, and after I pee. Means

I'm growing up--I'm somebody's hero
who's younger than I but I have few friends,
none, really, at school, which we live far from,
so I'm a role model for nobody
but the dog, who got run over last month.
So I have an imaginary friend
and she's a girl. One day we'll get married
because we like each other--I don't know
about sex yet, how it makes babies and

causes divorce. I meet my parents at
the fountain in front of the clothing store
an hour later. Father sits on the edge
of the little pool with the lights under
the water. Mother, smoking, stands over
him. *Well, sure thing*, Honey, he says. *You bet*.
I appear, and cough so they'll notice me.
It's like being born one more time except
I'm nine years old and not covered with blood
nor screaming, not that I remember that.
Hello, Son, they say. They say it as if

I'm the one thing that holds them together.
I'm like glue, I guess, but I don't smell bad.
I'm ready, I say. So are we, they say.
So we find our '65 Chevy II
--I crawl in and sit alone in the back
--and we drive home with the sun behind us
and it's setting. I'd read my comic book
but I get carsick. Anyway, I want
to save it for tonight, after the Braves
on the radio. Then I'm alone in
my attic bedroom with the Justice League.
I fall asleep and someone's asking me

if I'd like to join the group. You kiddin',
I say--where do I sign up? Then I
wake and my heroes are back in the book
and it's too late for serious reading

now anyway. Father and Mother go
to bed--I hear their door slam so I read
my comic, and all the ads, twice over,
and it's righteous and I'm going to be

like Superman, but no kryptonite, and
trounce evil if it's the last thing I do,
and outrun trains and stop bullets, and smoke.

The Blood
by Ben Crowley

1. No one can stop The Blood.

2. No one can know whether The Blood is good or bad.

The Blood wears a long red cape, so long it is like a power line snapped and hanging down to the ground. What is the process of The Blood?

To start, The Blood finds an unlocked door. He comes into your home. He learns the contents of your cabinets, the pills you need to take. He learns how your body works. He tries on your pants and your socks. He takes what he can get. He brings your things back to his black palace of darkness.

The black palace is a tall hill of stone and high color-stained glass depicting many strange knights with rare animals in unforseen states of life. For instance, the tale of one Salzburgian knight of silvery beard and moor-colored eyes who, kneeling in the gore of a stag slain for his love-ailing wife, was distracted a moment by a four-leafed clover, which he plucked, and hid away in his belt. It is inside the black palace, where the black candles burn, where The Blood blots the wine from his blackened red mouth, where The Blood draws his black curtains and pours in black darkness through black shelves of black books of red text on black pages.

The Blood wears a red suit, a red cape, red gloves, a red mask. Nightly he sits in his black bath which he does not fill with water, but let's fill with blood.

There was once a little girl The Blood saved on a fire escape in The Dumps of New York.

She was waiting for the end of parents' argument, which filled the apartment with a million broken bits which were hard to not touch.

She waited on her fire escape, as she had split her finger open and was holding it as hard as she could. She recalled what little poetry she could as distraction: "Then naked and white, all their bags left behind, they rise upon clouds, and sport in the wind. And the Angel told Tom, if he'd be a good boy, he'd have God for his father and never want joy."

The Blood loped up the fire escape and appeared. "Do you believe that crime exists?" he said.

"Yes," she said.

"And do you pray that we will one day live in a world where one day no crime will exist?"

"I pray it," she said.

He ducked under the low bars of the fire escape and took her hands up in his. They were full of dried blood and fresh red and now, with no pressure, watery rivulets wrapped her palms like silk ribbons. He kissed the bloody palms of her hands.

It was only up close that the victim of crime saw The Blood standing still, and that his eyes could be seen under The Blood's red satin mask. They were hideous eyes. To the little girl, like a doll come to life–but she could not take her hands away.

Four stories below in the dark, wretched alley, a pair of forty-five year old teenagers plunged the heroin in. Three interested cats slunk around their bare ankles, two of them black, and one of them gray.

The girl watched The Blood's mouth. The way his teeth were all pointed, his mouth like a leech, or the long piano keys of the carnival clown. When The Blood withdrew his dark mouth–how horrible, how endless–she wrenched back her healed hands. She turned them over. She looked for the wounds.

"Why are you super?" she said, as frightened as ever.

"If I were not super," said The Blood. "I would be only a

hideous monster."

The Blood flew into the night.

If ever you find yourself with a little scrape, a little cut, or little wound, The Blood will find a way through your window.

Wrath of a Druidess
by Audra Burwell

Down the moss-carpeted path you creep,
Dewdrops crunching between your toes,
Needles of ice embedded in callus.
Hands emerge from your tattered cloak,
The claws of a she-witch,
Gnarled and twisted, remains of a vile act.
Whorls of black ink gliding over skin,
Peek from beneath your veil,
Runic tattoos, symbols of power,
Dance across your peeling flesh,
Like a shadowy serpent emerging.
Eyes of cobalt pierce the atmosphere,
Cutting like a poison-tipped blade,
Revealing who you truly are.
An abomination to mankind.
A banished druidess, scorned and hurt,
You grasp your wrist,
Where the brand still burns red-hot.
How wrong they were,
To destroy the unknown,
To crush what they failed to understand,
The last flicker of magic,
Balancing on the tenuous horizon of yesterday.
Rage churns in your gut,
Liquid fire cascading and bubbling,
A potion for destruction evolving.
You stoop to pluck the bulb-capped fungi,
Sprouting wildly at your feet,
Ruby red spots dotting their pores,
Like glistening raspberries, poised to burst,
A sickly sweet poison,
Trapped in the veins of their folds.
You crush the delicate membrane,
Between spindly, razor-tipped fingers,
Watching the amber liquid pool in your palm,
Tasteless, odorless, and subversive.
The downfall of a kingdom,
Once gilded and magnificent,
Lies in your hands.

Nancy Drew Among the Amazons

by Kate Falvey

There's a story in this, girls,
and it doesn't have any wolves

in it for now, though you never know
what might come down the lane,

in Neverland, especially near
that mermaid bog of old.

Which is the gateway to
Themyscira, truth be told,

though no one ever seems
to want to know

where the Lost Girls go
after we fall, nanny's eyes

misty and indulgent
on the showboating boys,

meaning fewer of them end up
bait for the croc and the hook

and Peter's tricky ego
and more of them grow up

to prowl the regular streets,
sharpening claws on the regular air.

So when my poor distracted
daddy left me alone outside

the frosted panels of his legal
office door, I fussily pitched

over the side of my pram,
though I like to think that

natural curiosity gave me
a boost and a leg up.

Then plunk
in the iridescent waters

fizzing with wails and tails,
the sidewalk melting

into mermaids
who dragged me down

to the depths where I
apparently needed to be,

and I floated on their singing
to the hidden shore

of the women warriors
who trained me to keep

and uncover secrets,
to know which to guard,

which to expose,
and how to track clues

to the lairs of the everyday
demons and outwit them

before they claim and defile
another hallowed grail.

No One is Wise -- Possible Magical Antidote #1
by Farnilf P.

No one is wise. Smart people do not pull the strings.

Strings are being pulled. An invisible hand, sculpted and programmed to accumulate wealth and power, maintains the show. Agents of billionaires keep the mechanisms running, wheels greased, think tanks churning.

Money flows where needed. When the hand sweeps, the rich reap more. Dreams get funneled. Alternatives gaslit.

No one is wise.

Money decides, it's true, as far as words go. They echo against the wall. The machine churns us all forward together, regardless, closer to the edge. We can see the abyss, but we cannot turn the machine, or so they say.

So here's some decent TV for once. Stay out of our invisible hand's business. Instead, beware the enemies, remember to hate.

Money decides. No one is wise.

We've been trained from birth to expect the hero, the superhero. That god on earth who will defeat the monster hand, turn the wheel, save us all.

Well, it's all fine and good to engage in magical thinking, for fun and relief, but quite a bad idea to stake your survival on it.

We should all hope that Joseph Campbell had it very

wrong. He called the hero's journey the monomyth -- the one and only myth, all else being iteration. Could it be instead that this view dominates our story factories primarily as it is so very convenient to the hierarchy of wealth the hand has built?

In place of the communal myths -- the myths of strength through love and acceptance of the widening rings, webs and cycles of interconnected life -- a suffering hero returns, transformed by the ordeal. The action movie bible then impels the hero to commit great and righteous violence.

A thousand faces, a thousand screens, a thousand other myths shoved aside.

Money decides. No one is wise. Long past time to re-mythologize.

Mystique Exposed
by Phyllis Hemann

When I slam on the brakes,
I plunge headlong into
a proverbial brick wall,
nothing is the same.

My figure sprawls on the ground
stunned, unable to access
my abilities.

I submit my body
to rigorous testing
to locate my Achilles' heel.

All these tests
and treatments
do not empower me,
improve function.

I am weak, curled
in the fetal position

identical to Wonder Woman
when I left her behind,
speeding toward legacy.

I was strong
then. I needed not
her or anybody,

only my own agency
to conquer the planet
with fortitude belonging
merely to me.

Now I'm outside
and she's perched
in the driver's seat

of my weathered SUV.

I can only hope
she lassos me
and pulls me out
of this ditch.

The Golden Bureaucrat
by Bob Selcrosse

THE GOLDEN BUREAUCRAT, to this day, has saved 1,423 lives. What is the count for other heroes? We do not know. But we know how many deaths they have caused.

Black Widow: 48

Hulk: 65

Batman: 75

Wolverine: 101

Thor: 393

Captain America: 14,098

Superman: Uncountable

But THE GOLDEN BUREAUCRAT is an inverted hero. His secret identity does the heroism, all on the thirty-fourth floor. In his black second-hand suit, in his cubicle, he calls them up on the phone. He is a debt collector, but reminds every caller that all is not lost, that he appreciates their business, and that it is a beautiful day.

Only at home and off duty does he regain his true identity: THE GOLDEN BUREAUCRAT. He turns off the lights and reveals in the darkness his superman suit of crimson with brilliantly bright golden gloves, outside undies and unsurpassable goggles. It is finally, as he buttons the golden cape at his shoulders, that he takes from the freezer a gallon of Cherry Garcia, which he eats to completion and weeps at his life as a government employee.

Shining like lamplight in the dim black apartment, every morning he slips on his black suit and takes the city bus back to the office.

Mother Flood
by Anna Laura Falvey

In part, our cellar is a well.
When the ground swells,

pregnant with ocean brine
and rain, the water rises:

murky and dustclotted,
filtered through groundfloor

pores. In part, I remember
my mother downstairs in the slow,

slow, steady tide, I remember her
wildness, brave and rockjawed

in the face of her house, her house's
betrayal. Supposed to keep her safe,

keep her child safe, her house. I sit
upstairs in this memory, oreo creme

for dinner. The walls vibrate, whistle
in the wind: a howling like a monster's

mother wrapping her palms in fists
around each of our four walls. I scrape

creme off each cookie with my bottom teeth
and stack them in front of me: cairns, light-

houses, a tower of protection from the storm's
rage. My mother beats out the rising water

with sheer battlewill while from behind my tower
I rip sheets of newspaper, magazine scraps, grocery

lists, and sheets from the yellowpages: folding
paper boats to sail along the rocking waves.

Context is Everything
by Karla Linn Merrifield

He's having a rough, rough time, dementia diminishing him.
Tomorrow, a hospital bed arrives
on the scene, set up in the living room…he's lost his appetite just shy of totally; refuses much,
ergo not getting nearly enough nutrition no matter how hard I try…so he sleeps to conserve
energy…also tomorrow a geriatric social worker visits to work up a care plan based on needs
assessment, etc.…a no-copay Medicare health care aide now helps 3 days a week, 2 hours per…I
supplement with paid home aides. As his is a palliative-care, pre-hospice case, the goals are:
keep us both comfortable, help him stay at home.

Stylish hospital
gowns via Amazon Prime—
"Caretaker's Helper®"

I forge on: The cabin is going up! Foundation in, east wall half up. Library almost done with but
a few touch ups along baseboards for Andy the Handyman (whose wife's one of my health aides;
she works off the records, so earns 2x her Angels in the Home pay and I pay 25% less than
Comfort Keepers for much better care).

I hung multicolored (aqua, lime green, orange) tiki lights along the window (woodlands-facing),
moved a wooden 78s record-album cabinet (its provenance a long story), draping it with 2
color-compatible filmy cotton Indian head wraps, a sari accessory I'm thinking, $5 per at the
public market.

Last, I unpacked the last box of books, #78. In it, on top, was something I've never seen before.
It must have come from Roger's pre-Karla collection, must have

been one of the boxes he packed
for the move three years ago when he'd been able. There on top
was a message he sent me from
the Universe for when this day arrived.

From D.C. Comics:
Wonder Woman conquering
monster ships of death.

I'm not Her, but every day I work miracles.

The Book-Stellar and Cat-a-log concept art
unarchived by Mickey Collins

Unknown artist

Silver Age of Comic Books? (1956-1970)

Pencil on paper

Recently recovered art dating from around the Silver Age of Comics, these sketches show concept art of a previously unseen and unused superhero: The Book-Stellar and their sidekick/bookstore cat Cat-a-Log (following page). From the notes gathered, this was to be a superhero bookseller who gained superpowers when a bookshelf collapsed on them while they were reshelving a book on clichés. The artist's margin notes transcribed below from top left to bottom right:

Pointing to book on face, which served as superhero's mask: *Too heavy!* ~~Hardcover~~ *paperback*

Pointing to hyphen in The Book-Stellar: *hyphen - important!*

Noted near The Book-Stellar's mind waves: *More squigles?* [sic] & *Can read minds!* [*Ed. Note:* This power was meant for information-gathering purposes, such as guessing what book a customer was incorrectly describing.]

Middle-left: *Muscles!* [*Ed. Note:* Muscles were important during the Silver Age of Comics, even for a bookseller-based hero.]

Pointing to cape: *Cape made from mass market pages.* [*Ed. Note:* In the script, since lost to a fire, the Book-Stellar created their cape from the pages of books that had fallen out from reading them so much.]

Far-right: *Reaches overstock with ease!* [*Ed. Note:* Able to stretch limbs to reach the highest shelves.]

Bottom-left: *hands - later* [*Ed. Note:* hands are hard to draw.]

Unknown artist

Silver Age of Comic Books? (1956-1970)

Pencil on paper

Unused concept art of Cat-a-Log (or CaL), the Book-Stellar's bookstore cat turned into a plant-animal hybrid through unknown means. (No surviving script or marginalia described exactly how a cat and a log became one, but readers probably wouldn't have cared to know anyways.) CaL's powers would include an encyclopedic knowledge (which would be shared with the reader through sarcastic thought bubbles, a la Garfield) and the ability to shed pages when it scratched itself.

The artist's margin notes transcribed below from top left to bottom right:

Note on CaL's body: *Insert log texture here* [*Ed. Note:* the log texture (bottom-right) was to be used on top of C-a-L's body before sending the final art to print.]

Near CaL's tail: *fur? wood?*

Top-right: *Rings = age* referring to rings of a tree indicating the tree's age.

Pointing to CaL's asterisk butthole: *Very important*

Middle-left: ~~DogWood?~~ [*Ed. Note:* Scrapped name for CaL, if it was a dog instead of a cat.]

Bottom-middle: *How sit?* [*Ed. Note:* The writer never wrote a scene where CaL would be sitting for this very reason.]

Bottom-right: [*Ed. Note:* What if CaL had a monocle?]

Bios

Gale Acuff

I have had poetry published in *Ascent, Reed, Journal of Black Mountain College Studies, The Font, Chiron Review, Poem, Adirondack Review, Florida Review, Slant, Arkansas Review, South Dakota Review, Roanoke Review*, and many other journals in a dozen countries. I have authored three books of poetry: *Buffalo Nickel, The Weight of the World*, and *The Story of My Lives*.

Vincent A. Alascia

Vincent A. Alascia is the author of, "The Hole In Your Mind," "Undead Heart," "In the Presence of Gods," and, "Xristos: Chosen of God," available on Kindle and paperback as well as works that have appeared in anthologies and online. Originally an East Coast native, he makes his home in the Portland Oregon area with his wife. Vincent has been a librarian for over 15 years and is also a musician. He is currently working on a Steampunk Horror novel and a guide to reading Tarot. Website: www.vaalascia.com

Maev Barba

Dr. Maev Barba attended the Puget Sound Writer's Conference in 2018. She is a PNW native and a great lover of books. She used to sell books door-to-door. A doctor of astronomy, Barba looks into space and considers neither the small as too little, nor the large as too great, for the lover of stars knows there is no limit to dimension.

Audra Burwell

Audra Burwell is a creative writing major with a strong emphasis on fantasy-themed poetry and fiction that covers universal subject matter. She studies at California State University Fresno where she is aiming for a Master of Fine Arts degree. She is currently employed by Fresno State's Kremen Department as a Communications Assistant where she designs articles, media advisories, website content, press releases, and flyers that advocate for numerous college programs and that promote the student body on campus. She also simultaneously works for A Book Barn in Old Town Clovis and for their sub-business, HBE Publishing, where she has held a position for over six years. There, she performs a variety of tasks including clerical responsibilities, social media administration, inventory management, book design, editing, and event planning. Some of Audra's hobbies include archery, photography, snowboarding, skydiving, horseback riding, cosplaying, and traveling.

Avary Clemont
I'm Avary, an 18-year-old fantasy writer from Florida. I love writing books and hope to get published someday. My biggest inspirations are Lev Grossman, Stephen King, and Walter Tevis, to name a few.

Mickey Collins
Mickey ~~rights wrongs~~. Mickey ~~wrongs rites~~. Mickey writes words, sometimes wrong words but he tries to get it write.

Ben Crowley
Ben Crowley is from Pittsburgh, Pennsylvania. He is happy to get back to writing because he has already paid a kidney, three molars, a finger and a thumb to Deep Overstock and is weighing the value of his sensory organs. Ben used to sort books for the Amazon warehouse, in our beautiful backcountry of western Pittsburgh.

Doug
"doug" has been writing and drawing all their life. They found it was time to come out of their cave and share some of these creations. "doug" may or may not be a pseudonym for a person who works at a prolific Northwestern local bookstore, but feels the name "doug" represents their works just as samely as any other old name.

Patricia Dutt
I work as a landscape estimator in Ithaca, NY and although I am not a librarian, I visit the library often and read 52 books last year.

Lynette G. Esposito
Lynette G. Esposito, MA Rutgers, has been published in *Poetry Quarterly*, *North of Oxford*, *Twin Decades*, *Remembered Arts*, *Reader's Digest*, *US1*, and others. She was married to Attilio Esposito and lives with eight rescued muses in Southern New Jersey.

Robert Eversmann
Robert Eversmann works for *Deep Overstock*.

Anna Laura Falvey
Anna Laura Falvey (she/her) is a Brooklyn-based poet and theater-maker. In 2020, she graduated from Bard College with degrees in Classics & Written Arts, with a specialty in Ancient Greek tragedy and poetry. She spent her college career blissfully hidden behind the Circulation and Reference desks at the Stevenson Library, where she worked. Anna Laura has been a teaching artist with Artists Striving to End Poverty since 2019, with Lumina Theatre

Company since 2021, and will begin a teaching fellowship with ArtistYear in January of 2022. She currently works as editorial assistant at *Bellevue Literary Review*, and is currently serving as an ArtistYear fellow, teaching Poetry in Queens, NY.

KATE FALVEY

Kate Falvey's work has been published in many journals and anthologies in the U.S., Ireland, and the U.K.; in a full-length collection, *The Language of Little Girls* (David Robert Books); and in two chapbooks. She co-founded (with Monique Ferrell) and edited the *2 Bridges Review*, which was published through City Tech/CUNY, where she teaches, and is an associate editor for the *Bellevue Literary Review*.

PHYLLIS HEMANN

Phyllis Hemann grew up reading and telling stories. As a child, she scribbled poems with crayons. Now she writes her own for children and adults. She holds a M.F.A. from Antioch University Los Angeles. Her work has appeared in newspapers, journals and anthologies. She is the author of THE INVISIBLE HEROINE (Finishing Line Press). She lives in Arkansas with her family and their goofy dog. Find her online @phyllishemann and phyllishemann.com.

CJ HUNTINGTON

I've lived in the northwest about six months now and have been working at Powell's at Burnside since the fall.

LUCY JAYES

Lucy has fostered a love of writing since she was old enough to hold a pen. She graduated with a degree in English Literature from the University of Kentucky in 2014. During college, she interned for Ace Weekly magazine with a primary focus on covering local events and happenings in the food and beverage industry in Lexington. Upon graduating, she moved to Denver, CO and worked in nonprofit fundraising and event planning and as a conference manager and journalist for a trade magazine covering the legal cannabis industry. She is a first year MFA student at the University of Kentucky and focused on Creative Nonfiction writing.

WIT LEE

Wit lee, whose Chinese name is Li Hui, and pen name is Muzihuixin. She is a female poet born in Jining ,Shandong province, and now lives at the foot of Mountain Taishan. She is an editor of *Taishan University Journal*, a member of Taian Writer's Association and Taian Poets' Association. She has published more than 40 poems and one poetry book: *Beyond Time*.

Aurora Lewis

Aurora M. Lewis is a retiree, having worked in finance for 40 years. In her fifties, she received a Certificate in Creative Writing-General Studies, with Honors from UCLA. Aurora's recent poems, short stories, and nonfiction were accepted by *The Literary Hatchet, Jerry Jazz Musician, The Copperfield Review, Gemini Magazine*, to name a few. Now in her early70s, she self-published her first book, *Jazz Poems, Reflections on a Broken Heart* in 2021, which is available on Amazon. She is currently working on two collections of essays/poems, and speculative short stories.

Lance Manion

Lance Manion is the author of 10 short story collections, with an 11th being released in March. His writing has appeared in 50+ publications and a dozen anthologies. He has been posting content daily on his eponymous website for almost ten years.

Karla Linn Merrifield

Karla Linn Merrifield has had 1000+ poems appear in dozens of journals and anthologies, with 14 books to her credit. Following her 2018 *Psyche's Scroll* (Poetry Box Select) is the newly released full-length book *Athabaskan Fractal: Poems of the Far North* from Cirque Press. Her newest poetry collection, *My Body the Guitar,* inspired by famous guitarists and their guitars, was published in January 2022 by Before Your Quiet Eyes Publications Holograph Series (Rochester, NY). Website: www.karlalinnmerrifield.org. Blog at karlalinnmerrifeld.wordpress.com. Tweet @LinnMerrifiel

Jen Mierisch

Jen Mierisch's first job was at a public library, where her boss frequently caught her reading the books she was supposed to be shelving. Her work can be found in Fiction on the Web, Funny Pearls, Little Old Lady (LOL) Comedy, and elsewhere. Jen can be found haunting her local library near Chicago, USA. Read more at www.jenmierisch.com.

Timothy Arliss OBrien

Timothy Arliss OBrien is an interdisciplinary artist in music composition, writing, and visual arts. His goal is to connect people to accessible new music that showcases virtuosic abilities without losing touch of authentic emotions. He has premiered music with The Astoria Music Festival, Cascadia Composers, Sound of Late's 48 hour Composition Competition and ENAensemble's Serial Opera Project. He also wants to produce writing that connects the reader to themselves in a way that promotes wonder and self realization. He has published several novels (*Dear God I'm a Faggot,*

They), several cartomancy decks for divination (The Gazing Ball Tarot, The Graffiti Oracle, and The Ink Sketch Lenormand), and has written for Look Up Records (Seattle), Our Bible App, and Deep Overstock: The Bookseller's Journal. He has also combined his passion for poetry with his love of publishing and curates the podcast The Poet Heroic and he also hosts the new music podcast Composers Breathing. He also showcases his psychedelic makeup skills as the phenomenal drag queen Tabitha Acidz.
Check out more of his writing, and his full discography at his website: www.timothyarlissobrien.com

Farnilf P.
Farnilf P. is a member of a pseudonymous arts collective dedicated to world domination. An ephemeral art book of this work is forthcoming from PiNPRESS.online, and the author is in negotiations with Evil Portent Publishing for a children's picture book edition.

Viviann Ruiz
When Viviann Ruiz isn't working as a library assistant they can be found drawing either in their local park or at home. Taking artistic inspiration from movies and video games. Most of their art can be found at glynloryl@tumblr.com.

Bob Selcrosse
Bob Selcrosse grew up with his mother, selling books, in the Pacific Northwest. He is now working on a book about a book. It is based in the Pacific Northwest. The book is *The Cabinet of Children*.

Michael Santiago
Michael Santiago is a serial expat, avid traveler, and writer of all kinds. Originally from New York City, and later relocating to Rome in 2016 and Nanjing in 2018. He enjoys the finer things in life like walks on the beach, existential conversations and swapping murder mystery ideas. Keen on exploring themes of humanity within a fictitious context and aspiring author.

Rob D. Smith
Rob D. Smith is a common man attempting to write uncommon fiction in Louisville, KY. His work has appeared in *Apex Magazine, Shotgun Honey, The Arcanist, Thriller Magazine, Bristol Noir, Rock and a Hard Place Magazine, Tough*, and several other crime, horror, and speculative anthologies and online magazines. He co-hosts The Abysmal Brutes podcast that explores pop culture storytelling at theabysmalbrutes.podbean.com Follow him on Twitter @RobSmith3

E.T. Starmann
E.T. Starmann is a pulp fanatic. Although he may not be a professional bookseller or librarian, he is a long-time Weird Tales, Amazing Stories, AllStory collector. A Portland native, E.T. has spent countless hours in the Gold Room nook at Powell's, pouring through the latest pulp rack covers. E.T.'s work is heavily inspired by Lloyd Arthur Eshbach, Robert E Howard and Edgar Rice Burroughs.

Eric Thralby
Captain by trade, Cpt. Eric Thralby works wood in his long off-days. He time-to-time pilots the Bremerton Ferry (Bremerton—Vashon; Vahon—Bremerton), while other times sells books on amazon.com, SellerID: plainpages. He'll sell any books the people love, strolling down to library and yard sales, but he loves especially books of Romantic fiction, not of risqué gargoyles, not harlequin romance, but knights, errant or of the Table. Eric has not published before, but has read in local readings at the Gig Harbor Candy Company and the Lavender Inne, also in Gig Harbor.

Z.B. Wagman
Z.B. Wagman is an editor for the *Deep Overstock Literary Journal* and a co-host of the Deep Overstock Fiction podcast. When not writing or editing he can be found behind the desk at the Beaverton City Library, where he finds much inspiration.

Alex Werner
Alex is a lifelong reader and writer of stories. Raised on Arthur Conan Doyle and Agatha Christie, she found comics and superheroes later in life. Alex is a collector of books with inscriptions written to other people. She cherishes these books and their secrets. Contact @alexwerner20 on Twitter to contribute a book to the collection.

Nicholas Yandell
Nicholas Yandell is a composer, who sometimes creates with words instead of sound. In those cases, he usually ends up with fiction and occasionally poetry. He also paints and draws, and often all these activities become combined, because they're really not all that different from each other, and it's all just art right?
When not working on creative projects, Nick works as a bookseller at Powell's Books in Portland, Oregon, where he enjoys being surrounded by a wealth of knowledge, as well as working and interacting with creatively stimulating people. He has a website where he displays his creations; it's nicholasyandell.com. Check it out!

All rights to the works contained in this journal belong to their respective authors. Any ideas or beliefs presented by these authors do not necessarily reflect the ideas or beliefs held by Deep Overstock's *editors.*